The *Submissive* Cheerleaders

by Jordan Church

See what I have available and my author bio (such as it is) and photo (such as it is) at

amazon.com/author/jordanchurch

Feel free to contact me: jordanchurch@mail.com

Sign up for my newsletter to be notified of new releases as they occur. No waiting and wondering, just waiting! Also includes a sample scene from each new release for your enjoyment. Ctrl-click to open a hyperlink:

http://tinyletter.com/Jordan8Church

The *Submissive* Cheerleaders

Penny wanted to be taken seriously and wanted to be successful in life but so far circumstances seemed to have conspired against her.

The service industry sucked.

She had a spare moment after serving the last two huge orders, one for a family and the other for a raucous crew of men watching a Saturday evening college football game.

Penny had tables 4 thru 8 and, surprisingly, no one needed any drink refills. But she knew they soon would. They always wanted their bottomless drink/endless refill money's worth on those sodas.

Not that she blamed them. Money was so tight for her she'd given up drinks other than water from the faucet which was, of course, free. Except for here at Mack's Sports Bar and Eatery. The staff were allowed as much fountain soda as they wanted so she did get a break from water here. All free. One of the few perks of the job. The actual pay? Not a perk.

Penny figured management only let them have the perk of free soda in order to perk them up and get added work out of them.

Being stuck in a job like this made her cynical.

Penny loitered near the order pick-up window. She actually wished she didn't have a spare moment. Spare moments gave her time to think. When thought turned to her own circumstance in life it was pretty depressing.

Twenty-eight years old. A waitress. Having worked for years as a waitress she respected the hard work. Someone needed to do it. But she did have a degree in Psychology. Good grades, too.

Once she graduated, her temporary waitress job to help make ends meet became more and more long term. Numerous job interviews led to nothing. Nothing at all in her field. She took on more hours as a waitress.

After the half-year window closed between getting her degree and getting a job in her field her odds of getting such a job went way downhill. Then her one year window, a much smaller window, also closed. There were statistics on that, but, putting the math aside, the odds of actual employment in her actual chosen field could best be termed as "You're fucked".

Now she'd been a waitress for seven years, four of them more or less full time! With decades of possible waitress work stretching before her. It was depressing.

The tips were pretty good actually but any extra money went to paying off her college loan debts which were enormous.

No help from family. No family. Deadbeat Dad left the scene before Penny was even an adolescent. Mom died while she was in college.

Poor overworked Mom hadn't even gotten to see her graduate. Mom had been so proud of Penny's grades and her desire to help people. The bright side, such as it was, was that Mom didn't have to see her stuck spinning her wheels as a waitress.

No brothers or sisters either, not that she ever would have asked any for help if she did have them. She wasn't really a hardship case anyway, just not successful.

Why hadn't she gotten a position in her field, especially with her good grades? No one else was in the order pick-up area so Penny looked down at her chest. May as well. Everybody else did.

She could look at her breasts like everyone else did but she couldn't feel the same way about them. They were big. Not circus act big but pretty much the ideal size to a man (and to many women!). Which meant they were actually way too big. They looked out of place on her tall slim body.

She planned to have them surgically reduced. By at least half. Ironically they were so big they actually looked like they'd been surgically enhanced. Which was one reason why she wanted them surgically reduced. Ironically.

Also ironic: She would have used the money from her career in psychology (and the health insurance) to get the procedure done. Instead, her breasts were one of – well, two of – the reasons she did not get employment in her career field and could not afford to get them reduced.

Everyone who interviewed her thought she was too pretty and too stacked to be a good reflection on their practice. Of course, they didn't actually say that but she could see it in their eyes.

Some did hint at that reason. They asked how she would deal with patients who stared at her body. They asked how she'd deal with patients who she thought were ready to discontinue therapy but insisted on returning to see her again and again. They even asked how she planned to deal with stalkers!

She wanted to be wanted and hired for her ability and skill but she marveled that at none of the job opportunities did she ever run into anyone who wanted to hire her for her looks. For some forlorn hope of getting a date with her. Or just because they wanted to look at her around the office. But... nope... none of that. Her good looks (being honest, her great looks) did not assist her at all. Just the opposite.

By the time she figured it out and wore glasses and dowdy clothing to interviews she'd gone without employment in her field for a suspiciously long time making any hire a long-shot. Besides, concealing the massive shapes of her breasts wasn't really possible. The more you covered them the bigger they looked.

The Assistant Manager at Mack's, Esteban, startled her, "Taking a break?"

Esteban was a fucking asshole. To everyone, not just her. Drove all the waitresses like it was his job. Which it was but he was never satisfied and never had a kind word.

He never seemed like a manager type to Penny. What he lacked in height he made up for in scrawniness. With their height differential Penny looked down on him both figuratively and literally.

"Just catching my breath between orders, Esteban."

"You wanna extra break we can go hang out in my office."

That was how it was with Esteban. Always with the suggestive not-quite-sexual harassment. Well, it was, but good luck proving it. Report something like this and he'd just say he was being kindhearted to a waitress with aching feet. Even his tone was neutral. But his eyes. His face. Anyone would know what he really wanted.

"Thanks, but no thank you."

Esteban tried this kind of thing like clockwork. Pretty much every night. With all the waitresses. Refusals, polite or impolite, had no impact on the frequency of his vague propositions.

As far as Penny knew no one ever took him up on it. Then again, why would he spend so much time doing it unless it worked at least every once in a while? She did not keep track of what the other waitresses did on their breaks because she was so busy covering for them then.

Time for Estaban to drive her to do more work, "Better get back out there. No orders or whatever then just chat with those paying customers, make them think

you like them. Bat your eyes at them. Touch their arm while you talk to them.
Make sure they come back. Hey, they gonna tip you better too."

"Fine, Esteban. I'll get right on that."

She realized Esteban was staring at her chest while lost in thought.

Fucking asshole.

Penny went back out to her tables and one of the crew of men watching the
football game flagged her down. There were five of them sitting high up on bar stool
chairs around a big round table.

When he saw her coming their way he elbowed the men on either side of him
and all five looked at her expectantly.   They looked like they were trying to hold
back laughter.

Here we go, she thought. He'd told them he was going to make a pass at her
and they were going to watch with amusement. They had to know she'd shoot down
his advance. He was overweight and bald for God's sake and at least twenty years
older than her!

He also wore a wedding band. Another fucking asshole!

She arrived at the table, "How are you gentlemen doing? Anything I can get
for you?"

She even managed to keep sarcasm out of her tone as she said "gentlemen".

The first man, who she thought of as "Baldy", answered, "As a matter of fact, there is, sweetheart. I dropped a coin down there. Can you fetch it for me?"

Now all five of them looked at her with expectant amusement. She almost gave him the finger. Almost. She glanced over towards the kitchen.

There was Esteban blatantly watching her. She'd gotten in trouble before for standing up for herself. She was always told the customer was always right. Which was pure bullshit but true as the sun rising in the East to management.

Fuck it. Who cared. It wasn't worth trouble.

All this, the situational recognition, awareness of consequence, how it made her feel, and how she would handle it, passed through her quick mind in a fraction of second.

"Certainly, sir. Did you see where it landed?"

"Not really. Down there somewhere. Sort of dark in here. You might need to get down on hands and knees to spot it." A couple of his friends put hands on their mouths to stifle giggles.

These fucking assholes. Penny looked one more time at Esteban. He was frowning at her like he could tell she didn't want to do something the customers did want her to do. That fucking asshole also!

She leaned down even knowing they would be looking at her ass. She wasn't going to get down there and crawl around like he wanted!

Her dark brown wavy hair tumbled around her face. Great, now her hair was a mess.

She peered around the chair legs and the table support. She heard the inevitable innuendo talk from the five. It was obvious whenever they said "game" they were actually talking about her ass.

"Sure is a tight *game*, huh guys?"

Yeah, right, she'd seen the score was 31-14 half way through the third quarter!

"Oh, yeah, it's a great *game*!"

Yeah, right, she'd seen the score was 31-14 half way through the third quarter!

"That there is anybody's *game*."

Yeah, right, she'd seen the score was 31-14 half way through the third quarter!

"That *game* goes to whoever takes it. Whoever grabs it!"

Fucking assholes!

Penny saw the coin. It was a penny. A fucking penny! She realized they'd seen her name on her name-tag and concocted this scenario based on her name.

Thanks Mom and Dad, what a stupid name, she thought for the thousandth time. It was good she didn't have a brother or a sister. She was sure they would not have been any happier named Nickel and Dime.

She plucked up the penny and delivered it into the hand of #1 asshole.

Baldy winked at her, "So?"

"So what, sir?"

"Was it heads up or heads down?"

"I don't know, I didn't look."

Asshole #2 to Baldy's right leaned forward, "You have to look. You know why, right?"

Before she could answer Asshole #3 to Baldy's left also leaned forward talking like he was passing on the secret to life, "Because a penny heads up is good luck..."

Baldy finished his sentence as had obviously been planned, "... but a *Penny* head down is even better luck!" The emphasis on "Penny" informed her he definitely meant it with a capital P. As in Penny giving oral sex.

Fucking assholes!

One of the others chimed in as she tried to look calm and innuendo oblivious, "Know what I heard? I heard rub a *Penny* for good luck."

"I'd sure like to give that a try," said the last asshole of the five.

She saw Baldy was actively and suggestively rubbing the penny she'd just given to him.

"Anything else? *Gentlemen*?"

There wasn't. She wasn't surprised they didn't try to utilize the old "Penny for your thoughts" line. Guys like this wouldn't care what she thought.

When they finally left an hour later they left a deficient tip, less than 5%. Those fucks!

"How was your shift, Penny?"

"The usual."

"That bad, huh?"

"Yes, Lynn. That bad."

Waitresses didn't get to live on their own in their own house. It wasn't financially possible. So Penny had a roommate and they lived in an old paint-peeling apartment.

Lynn was also a waitress at Mack's which is where they'd met and what led to them being roommates though it was a recent development since Penny had been at Mack's much much longer than Lynn.

Lynn was nice enough but very different than Penny.

She was young, just twenty-one. Penny felt like an old lady compared to her.

Lynn was blonde while Penny was brunette.

She was short which made Penny feel even more awkwardly tall when standing next to her.

She had small breasts and sometimes seemed fascinated, almost worshipful, of Penny's big boobs.

And... she liked to run around their small downtown apartment wearing very little or sometimes even nothing. Which really really bothered Penny though she never said anything directly to Lynn. She always tried to get along.

She also seemed quite free with her body. In the two months they'd been rooming together probably eight times Lynn's volume levels during sex kept Penny awake or woke her up from sleep. The apartment had thin walls. Eight times with, apparently, eight different guys! It seemed Lynn liked variety.

Lynn was so different than Penny that Penny, though they'd had some fun times, kinda wished Lynn wasn't her roommate. Should she have asked Lynn before she moved in if she was going to bring home and fuck four different guys a month? In hindsight, yes, she should have.

Penny kicked off her shoes and flopped down on the slightly lopsided chair with the ripped upholstery that she and Lynn acquired when someone in their apartment complex chucked it in the dumpster. They had laughed and giggled as they dragged and rolled it up two flights of steps. Their efforts made it lopsided in a whole new direction.

Penny closed her eyes. She was beat.

An unknown number of minutes later she came alert from her drowsy state listening to the television. Something woke her fully. She felt something at her feet and looked down to see Lynn on her knees next to Penny one hand rubbing each of Penny's feet.

"What are you doing, Lynn?"

"Rubbing your feet, silly."

"They're stinky from me walking them all over Mack's for a shift."

"I don't mind."

Penny blinked away the sleep further. What the hell? It felt nice but it was sort of weird.

"You can stop, Lynn. I didn't ask you to do that."

"I like to help people feel good. I know how sore feet feel after a shift. You didn't ask me but I'm sure you like it."

"It's weird. No thank you. You can stop."

Lynn stopped but looked hurt, "It's not weird. Esteban likes it. So do some of the other waitresses."

"Esteban! He's an asshole. And twice as old as you. And married. When do you rub his feet?"

"In his office. He invites me back there. Some of the other waitresses too. Sometimes he lets us, well, tells us to rub each other too."

"Lynn! That is totally messed up!"

"You think that's messed up...."

"What? What were you saying?"

"Never mind."

"Lynn, you're too nice. You can't just go around trying to please everyone else. Especially assholes. It's not wise."

"Are you saying I'm dumb?"

Penny would never say that... to her face, "All I'm saying is, they take advantage and you get the short end of the stick."

Lynn's face took on a different look, sort of intent, "Actually I got the long end of the stick. Believe me."

"No! Tell me you did not let that creep fuck you!"

"Gee, I'd hate to lie to you like that...."

"What were you thinking?"

"I guess I thought it would make him happy. It did. Making others happy makes me happy too. Plus, it's a nice break at work. Sort of energizing."

"I can't believe this. He is totally taking advantage of you. He isn't even good looking!"

"Well, all cocks are ugly if you think about it but pretty much equal."

"Gross. Just gross. This is not good for you. Not just Esteban. That whole please others submissive thing. Not healthy at all."

Lynn used a sing-song voice, "You're wrooooong. Esteban gives me extra hours! As long as I share my tips with him."

"Share your tips? Lynn, you earn those tips. You rely on them. He has no right to them."

"Maybe but he also doesn't hassle me. Some time in his office and he is sweet as a lamb. For me its pretty much just an extra break. Unless me makes me orgasm. Then it's better."

"Lynn, listen to me, you can't be like this. Just giving in to assholes like him. You can't reward his bad behavior."

"I like making people happy and I do that with him."

"People take advantage of you. I mean, obviously. They just take and take as much as you let them and you get nothing in return."

"That isn't so true, Penny. I was waiting to tell you since you seemed so tired. But you look awake now. Guess what? I'm going to be a cheerleader! The way I got the job was by being willing to put up with a little grab-ass and some nasty talk. Whatever else. He said that's what got me the job."

"What? A cheerleader? What are you talking about? Some man grabbed your ass and you let him because he said he'd let you be his cheerleader?"

"No, silly, it wasn't like that. It's legit. They're opening a semi-pro football team. Well, it's sort of football. Some different rules. Anyway, they advertised for cheerleaders. I tried out and got on the squad. All because I didn't say anything when he got handsy and said some dirty things about what he'd like to do."

"Who did? Who is this creep?"

"Parker. Guy in charge."

"Parker? What's his first name?" Already Penny had a vague idea to go confront the guy.

"That is his first name. And his last name too! His name it Parker Parker if you can believe that."

"Not really. Did he show you ID?"

"No, but he's the real deal. The cheerleader coach was there, too. Real amazon type. It wasn't like this was in his apartment or something. It was at the stadium. They have it for games on Friday nights in the spring. Starting in a couple months but they have the money to fund a cheer team."

"He still sounds like an asshole. Just a legit asshole instead of a non-legit asshole."

"You think all the guys are assholes."

Penny shrugged slightly. That was pretty much true. Probably why she didn't have a boyfriend.

Lynn was rubbing her feet again! What was wrong with her?

Lynn continued, "If you met him you'd think he was a total nerd. Those little glasses, stripey suit, shorter than me. But he doesn't act like a nerd. He acts like... well, I guess you're right, he does act like an asshole. Still, I put up with him and I got the job."

"What about Mack's? I mean, fuck Mack's, but are you still going to work there?"

"I'll do both. But, hey, this job pays great and you get full four star health care too."

That caught Penny's attention, "Serious? Health care?"

"Yeah, no copay's or nothing. 100% coverage for every damn thing. I mean, I'm healthy but better safe than sorry."

"Wow. I see why you want the job."

"You should be on the cheer team with me!"

"What? No. Look at me."

"You're beautiful."

"Maybe so," Penny knew darn well there was no "maybe" to it, "but I'm not built to be a cheerleader even if I wanted to. My big boobs would flop all over the place."

"No, no. They like that sort of thing there. They want the cheerleaders to be like strippers wearing clothes. You know, semi-professional they need every edge they can get to get fans in the building."

"Like a stripper wearing clothing?"

"You should try out, Penny! They need more like me. That's exactly what Parker Parker said. So did Violet. She's the coach of the cheerleaders."

"Lynn, if they're looking for more just like you then they don't want me. If he put a hand on me I'd break a finger, then another, then another, until he apologized to me and all women everywhere."

"Penny, you don't have to actually be like me. Just *seem* to be like me. Go to the try out, ignore the touches and anything they say. Then, you get the job. I'll call in and set it up. Put in the good word for you."

This actually gave Penny pause. Get the job, wait for insurance to kick in, go get her procedure done. If she was being left alone after that, fine, she would have a new revenue stream. If not, break some fingers on a nerd/asshole with two last names. Or two first names. Or whatever.

The foot rub really did feel nice and relaxing. And, for whatever reason, Lynn really did seem to enjoy it. She was just so crazy eager to please. Lynn was so submissive! What a way to be. Always out to please everyone else instead of herself. No protective selfishness.

Fine, thought Penny, go ahead and knock yourself out, Lynn. Rub my feet all you want!

Penny fell asleep with Lynn still rubbing her feet.

━━━━━━━━━━━━━━━━━━━━━━━━━━━━━━━━━━━━━━━

Parker Parker and Violet were exactly as advertised and quite the oddball pair.

Penny wasn't sure if it was the same suit Parker Parker wore at Lynn's try out but it certainly was quite stripey. Three different colors!   Violet, the cheerleader coach, would look at home in a breast plate and holding a shield and a spear. She seemed like an odd fit as cheerleader coach. She was in Olympic great shape but no way had she ever been a cheerleader herself.

The try-out was just Penny and three other young women. She had no idea why an executive like Parker Parker would be involved at all. Well, based on his intent stares at tits and asses she had *some* idea. She just didn't know how he justified it assuming he had any supervision in his role.

Right from the start she thought she did well. Sadly, that was only because Parker's eyes were fixated on her. Specifically, her tits. Well, he could join the club. She got that reaction from all men. Like she was tits who happened to also have a human being attached to them.

Parker and Violet were an odd pair but they did have something in common. They both were fans of female anatomy. It was obvious to Penny that Violet was either bisexual or outright gay.

Parker and Violet both stared intently, eyes flicking from one candidate to the next, as all four were ordered, of all things, to do jumping jacks.

Penny hated how her breasts bounced and shook while doing the jumping jacks. Parker and Violet clearly loved it.

After thirty jumping jacks – which, proved what? – Violet then told them to touch their toes while standing. They were told to hold the pose while Violet moved around them just a couple feet away and Parker also circled but did so from further away. Like they were two planets in differing orbits circling a sun. Except, in this case, more like they were in orbit around the four moons of their asses.

One of the candidates straightened and stated, "I'm out of here."

And she was. Off she went.

Penny knew she herself also would have left at that point if she hadn't somewhat known what to expect from what Lynn told her. Lynn told her if she wanted the job she had to be the opposite of her real self. Which meant putting up with shit.

They lost the second candidate three exercises later when Violet told them all to do something called the open leg rocker. It was basically balancing your butt on the floor with head and feet up looking like a V from the side. Then holding ankles and spreading your legs to make a V that way as well. Which was damn hard on the ass and hard to do unless you had perfect balance.

Besides being physically awkward it was emotionally awkward to have those two staring at their stretched crotches.

The second candidate simply mumbled "Fuck this", grabbed her stuff, and was out of there as well.

After a few more really embarrassing positions there were still two of them left. Penny and a skinny blonde similar to Lynn. Penny wasn't sure how many spots were open. Maybe only one.

Hopefully they liked some variety in their line up of cheerleaders. This girl looked a lot like Lynn whereas Penny was very different other than being equally attractive.

The whole time Parker Parker stared from the fringes of his Neptune orbit. His suit looked too big for him, like he took it out of his father's closet. His pants, however, looked too small for him. Around the crotch.

Penny felt disgusted with the whole situation. She felt like a stripper who forgot to take off her clothes. At any moment she expected Parker to start throwing dollar bills at her.

Violet guided the two of them to a small nearby room where they were, rather surprisingly, given a test to take. Why hadn't Lynn warned her there would be a test?

The reason became pretty clear pretty quick though. The questions were silly. Things like her favorite color, her favorite animal, her favorite ice cream, her favorite food, her favorite one digit number, her favorite two digit number, her favorite season, her favorite month, her favorite holiday.

About forty questions like that. The last one asked her to imagine a horse out in the wild then write down it's description and exactly what she pictured it doing if she took a single photo of it.

Penny wondered how even one of those questions could reflect on a person's qualifications to be a cheerleader. At least those humiliating exercises showed some fitness and flexibility.

Violet collected the completed tests, quizzes, surveys, or whatever the hell they were. She and Parker huddled in the corner for a minute absolutely pouring over them like they were Archaeologists that just found two new scriptures accidentally left out of the bible.

Violet told the other girl to wait where she was sitting and told Penny to come with her. Penny followed her into an adjoining room and saw Parker Parker going into the room right next to it.

Violet closed the door and right away got up in Penny's face. Penny backed away. She couldn't help herself. Violet grinned but it wasn't a friendly grin.

"Do not move." Violet came back into her personal space. The inner boundaries of her personal space as Violet's breasts were only a hair away from rubbing up on Penny's own breasts. This time Penny managed not to back away.

"Cheerleaders cheer on the team but their real use is to entertain. With your body and smiles. Pretty much a stripper with some limited clothing on. Your attitude needs to be the same as a stripper."

Somehow Penny managed to say nothing.

"Your eyes must say you are grateful you are being looked at and enjoyed. Your smile must say you are happy to be ogled. Everyone is a customer and the customer is always right."

There is was again! More "customer is always right bullshit"! Penny felt like asking what if the customer claims two plus two equals one hundred and ninety-seven. You could bet your ass if the customer said they didn't have to pay for a meal or for game tickets management wouldn't think they were right then!

Penny held her retort inside.

"No matter what happens you smile and even say thank you. Someone calls you a sexy cunt you say "Why, thank you so very much kind sir or madam." Can you do that?"

Penny really wondered if she could. Would it really be like that? Right then was no time to show doubt, "Yes, Violet, I can."

"Let's put that to the test."

Penny had no idea what that meant.

For about half a second.

Violet walked behind her and slapped her ass.

Slapped. Her. Ass!

The act and the pain shocked Penny into immobility.

"Very good! Going to and from the lockers you pass by fans. Sooner or later one will spank you like that. Or at fan events they will. When they do, don't just stand there with your mouth open. It should be open but words should come out. The right words. Go ahead, what will you say to the money-paying highly valued fan when he spanks your perfect ass?"

"Ummmm. Thank you for spanking me?"

"Good. You could do better though. Engage in playful banter. You could say "Thank you, sir, but I hope your hand is not sore. I apologize if it is."

What the fuck! The sheer outrage was making Penny blink like a computer on the fritz.

"Here. Let us practice."

Before Penny could compute what that comment entailed another smack landed on her derriere. Harder this time and she took half a step forward to catch her balance. It was more difficult to catch her mental balance.

Penny looked at Violet when she circled back in front of her. Violet had an expectant expression on her face.

Oh. Yeah, right. What was she supposed to say again?

"Thank you, sir, hope your hand isn't sore. Sorry."

"Do I look like a "sir" to you?"

"No! Gosh no! I thought we were role-playing."

"Let's try it again then."

Oh shit!

Violet went back behind her and Penny actually had to bite her lip to keep from saying anything. The wait for the spank, even though it was only moments, seemed like an hour.

Smack!

Whoa! That one was even harder! Much harder!

Violet came back around and Penny said the words again this time using "ma'am" instead of "sir".

Violet smiled a tolerant amused smile, "Better. You think only men will spank that ripe ass of yours? Get real. Don't be such a sexist. You and your stereotypes. We don't like sexists around here. We like very polite sexy cheerleaders. Not sexist cheerleaders. It's a big difference."

"I understand."

"I don't think you do. But I'll give you a chance to prove me wrong. Tell me, being a polite little cheerleader, if a fan touches your tits, what will you say? Will you say "Thanks for noticing my boobs?" How about that?"

"I guess so. Yeah, that would work. Playful banter, right?"

"All right then, lets see if you are a sexist. Simple test."

Penny's eyes got real big as Violet stepped towards her. Violet reached out with both hands – both hands! – and firmly grasped both of her breasts. Or, at least, as much of them as she could contain even in her big hands.

Violet squeezed them rhythmically like they were giant-size stress relief balls.

Penny wondered when she was going to stop.

Penny wondered when she herself would put a stop to this and walk out.

But Penny had already put up with so much. She hated to waste all that effort. She also had something to prove to Violet apparently. She didn't want the amazon to think she was a sexist.

So she told herself.

Penny finally realized Violet would keep squeezing her boobs until she took her own cue. Which she better do as soon as possible.

What Violet was doing – and Penny knew, just knew, this was only a purely a physiological reaction – was having an effect on her.

Her damn nipples were getting stiff. Which was a problem because they were big, a good match to her big breasts, and they were way too sensitive. Once they got hard... yep, dammit, she was even getting wet. Fuck!

Penny spoke very fast, "Thank you for noticing my boobs, ma'am."

Violet hooded her eyes while still squeezing, "You are welcome, little slut."

Violet finally released them. Penny felt like she could breath again. Like Violet had been squeezing her actual lungs.

Slut?

Penny blurted out angrily before she could stop herself, "Slut? Did you call me a slut?"

"Yes, I did call you a slut. Many others will. All the honest ones. The liars will call you lady. Whatever you are called – slut, whore, bitch – you must always act like it is a great compliment and you are grateful for the kind recognition."

Penny realized her reaction was that of her real self and therefore the wrong one. Lynn would not have been insulted by being called a slut. Penny had even heard Lynn refer to herself that way though Penny had always hoped it was done jokingly. After what Lynn told her or at least hinted to her about what she did with Esteben it didn't seem like a joke.

Penny knew she had to act like Lynn. Like an eager to please slut. She could not afford to let herself slip from that role.

These spanks and amazonian boob grabs were nothing. Mind over matter. It didn't matter compared to breaking free from the service industry so she should not mind. Or at least pretend like she did not mind. She could not afford to let this get to her.

"I'm sorry, I just couldn't hear you what you said at first. I am a bit of a slut.

How did you know?"

Violet smiled indulgently. Violet clearly appreciated her willingness to debase herself, "I know you're a real slut because of your big tits. If there is a creator I sure as Hell hope she wouldn't waste tits like that on someone who wasn't a slut."

Penny wasn't at all sure how to respond to that so she stayed quiet.

"All right, you might just do. Go next door to Mr. Parker and tell him I said it's up to him. On the way tell that other slut to get her skinny ass in here."

"Oh. What's her name?"

"Don't know, don't care. To me she's just slut number two."

"That makes me number one slut. Yay! I'm the best!"

"There you go, slut number one. Playful banter."

Violet spanked her rear as she went past and the spank was hard, not at all playful. Penny very carefully did not react and kept walking.

Outside the office she felt like she'd escaped.

Turned out slut number two's name was Liana. Penny watched her go into the room with Violet and felt sorry for her.

She maybe should have saved that sympathy for herself. She went into the room with Mr. Parker. There was a desk and he had both feet up on it while he leaned back precariously in the swivel office chair. He held an open smart phone in front if him and seemed preoccupied reading whatever was on the screen.

She couldn't tell what he was looking at as he kept the back of it pointed at her so she could never see the screen and kept it that way.

"Mr. Parker. Violet says it is up to you."

"That's nice. Violet is such a treasure to our organization. She has an interesting history. She used to be a professional female wrestler. Her stage name, get this, was Violent Violet. Nice one, huh?"

"Yes, sir."

"Hard to say it five times fast though."

"I'm sure."

"Go ahead. Say it five times fast."

"Violent Violet, Violent Violet, Violent Violet, Violent Violet, Violent Violet."

"Very good oral skills. We like our cheerleaders to have the very most excellent oral skills."

If the words hadn't already told her this was innuendo, his tone made it certain. What a creep!

"Do you even know what team you are trying out to be a cheerleader for?"

She did. But only because Lynn had told her, "The Rhinos."

"Did you know that "Rhinos" is short for Rhinoceros?"

"Yes, sir." Penny thought maybe Parker was testing her to learn her level of self-control when confronted with stupid questions.

"Did you know that "Rhino" is also a term for the male equivalent to the female cougar. An older man looking to engage in sex with a younger woman, much younger?"

"Yes, sir." Now it was obvious to Penny that Parker was testing her to learn how she dealt with uncomfortable terms and subjects.

"I'm curious, what is the oldest man you would consider having sex with? Forty? Fifty? Senior citizen?"

Now she knew he was trying to see how she reacted when put on the spot, "Age is just a number."

She purposely chose not to add she'd look for someone with inner maturity who treated her with respect. That obviously would not go over well.

Parker nodded and smiled at her over the top of his smart phone, "That's a perfect answer."

Her honest answer would have been maybe ten years older. Outside chance? Maybe fifteen years older. Definitely at least a year less than whatever age Parker was.

Parker looked her up and down with no discretion and no shame whatsoever. At least he seemed pleased with what he saw. The tent at the groin of his pants seemed to expand.

Penny was glad she was doing well. She promised herself she'd maintain her air of eager-to-please and willing-to-do-anything. She'd come this far. Just a little further. She had to play this role like an actress.

"The Rhinos are a new team, a founding team, in a new kind of football. Sort of like how Arena Football League is similar but different. But Arena is a passing league. We go the other direction. We're a running league. Three downs to gain 5 yards. But if you don't make it in the first two runs you punt, of course. There is a lot of strategy because each team can pass but only seven times a game. You need to save your passes for desperate times to come from behind but you also want to use them when the other team does not expect it. Thus... strategy. Only seven players on the field at a time for each team. Saves on expenses."

Parker tilted his head to one side of the smart phone, "Do you even understand traditional football and these differences I've outlined?"

Penny barely bit back a smart-ass reply. He was so patronizing! But, no, she needed to own this role. She had to be like Lynn, "Yes, sir, I'm a waitress at a sports bar and grill and have picked up the rules."

Parker nodded, "Let's just check to make sure Violet did her job correctly and you are a good addition to the cheer team."

"Yes, sir."

"A good cheerleader, in out view, needs to be willing to bend over backwards to please."

"Yes, sir."

"Are you?"

"Yes, sir."

"Cheerleaders, when you boil it down, are there to please and please with their body. Am I correct?"

"Yes, sir."

Penny was very focused on playing her role perfectly. Lynn, and women like her, would eagerly and automatically agree. Penny was determined to agree or to do everything the exact same Lynn would.

It felt like her mind had a sort of "tunnel vision". She was blocking out entire fields of view to enable her role.

"All right then. Time to prove it. I want you to go ahead and bend over backwards. Physically. Hands and feet all on the ground."

Penny hesitated but it was only because she was not even sure she knew how to go about getting in the position. She did not let her mind entertain if this request was appropriate. Lynn wouldn't have so neither would she.

"Fans of our game are mostly men. As you can imagine, they love seeing sexy women bend themselves into pretzel shapes or bend over backwards and offer their female treasures to the sky. We plan to have the whole cheer team doing this kind of thing on the sidelines during the games."

It was clumsy but Penny adopted the requested pose. She didn't picture herself until after she was in the position. Her crotch was pretty much her highest point! Her big breasts despite the restraining top still slid down and crowded her chin. Her top slid down and exposed her bare belly and belly button.

"Spread you legs more. As much as you can." Parker's voice sounded thick with... emotion.

Penny was shocked by the request even though she shouldn't be by then. She immediately slid her feet apart while her leg and arm muscles trembled.

She heard Mr. Parker scrape his chair back and move around the desk. She realized the suited nerd creep was standing very close, right between her legs. If not for their respective clothing he could just lean forward and penetrate her. That thought, for no good reason, made her stupid pussy dampen.

"A lot of men, fans, highly valued fans, will want to touch you. Professional teams don't put up with that. But we're only semi-pro. We need every edge we can get. Cheerleaders wearing less. Cheerleaders in sexy positions. And, cheerleaders letting them do a little harmless touching. No big deal. Just let them touch."

Penny's position hid her face from Mr. Parker and she was glad it did. It would have shown too much angry disbelief even through her Lynn persona disguise. She also couldn't see Parker which was probably good because she knew he was almost certainly staring at her stretched crotch. That pervert!

"There is only one way to test if a cheerleader will do all they need to do to be successful with us. Too many little liars out there. So. Just pretend I'm an admiring fan."

Penny's eyes widened from worried shock and from all the blood rushing to her head. Her head was just over the carpet and her hair was actually brushing the carpet. Filthy!

She used concern for carpet lint sticking to her hair to help distract her from what Parker obviously planned to do. She didn't know exactly what he'd do but his words told her more or less what he intended.

She felt a hand on her knee. It gave a light squeeze.

Then she felt a hand on her bare tummy. A finger dipping into her navel. It kept sliding in and out of her navel. She suddenly realized he was pretending his finger was a tiny cock and her navel was a tiny pussy!

Why did that realization make her nipples harden?

Then that hand slid up her body. Which was to say it actually slid downwards towards her breasts. He did it slowly as if he was trying to give her time to react and object. She was determined not to be found out for the strong independent woman she was.

After all, on some level, he was right. Harmless touching. No big deal. It was all in the mind. You just had to not mind.

She didn't really think he'd do it anyway. A knee or a belly button? No big deal. But everyone knew touching a woman's breasts was wrong. Except under certain circumstances of course and this wasn't one of those.

Penny learned Parker had a different set of "certain circumstances".

His hand... was at her right breast... feeling it... fondling it... squeezing! Then it moved over and did the same to her left breast. Her left breast was even more sensitive then her right. Always had been. She thought it was because it was closest to her heart. But, in this case, it might also be because that nipple had hardened even more while he fondled her right breast.

This was crazy!

She could feel him press himself against her held-aloft hip. It was obvious his cock was as hard as her nipples. That pervert! But... what did that make her?

His hand moved to the top of her left breast and tweaked that nipple. Then it moved over and tweaked the right one.

Now the hand moved back up – or down – her body. Up physically, down figuratively. Right up her midriff towards her....

Was he... was he going to...!?!

He was.

His hand cupped and encompassed her pussy. She was suddenly aware, probably at the same time as Parker, that her pussy was quite wet. When did that happen?

His hand fondled her pussy. He made no secret of it. Just pushed and rubbed on it. Just helped himself. She couldn't believe he was doing it. She couldn't believe she was letting him. She couldn't believe how wet and needy her pussy was.

Stand up and leave now? It would mean he got to cop a free feel. She had already put up with so much. She couldn't waste that effort. That strange progress. It couldn't all be for nothing. If she left now then she'd get nothing out of all this!

No extra money. No fantastic health insurance. No breast reduction.

No orgasm.

Whoa. Where did *that* thought come from?

But she knew *exactly* where *that* thought came from....

As if being bent over backwards to please him both figuratively and literally wasn't enough, wasn't humiliating enough, he just had to twist the knife.

"What's your name again? Penny, right? Apparently you've had quite a workout with your try-out. You're so sweaty down here."

That... disgusting pervert! He had to know it wasn't sweat. But what was she going to do? Correct him? Tell him "Oh no, sir, that isn't sweat, it's my pussy juice flowing because how you're treating me is turning me on?" No way could she correct him. Never ever.

Besides, he already knew.

His hand aggressively worked on her pussy, really indenting her outfit into her pussy, making it soak even more, "I'm concerned, Penny. A little try-out has you this sweaty? You may not be in good enough shape to be a cheerleader here. If that is sweat I'm feeling...."

Damn him! He was intentionally trying to make her say it, to tell him it was pussy juice and not sweat. Just to humiliate her! Forcing her to say what she had just told herself she wouldn't. Never ever. She went from never ever to about to say it just because he said a few sentences.

Also because the blood was rushing to her head so she couldn't think straight. That's what she would tell herself later. She'd have to conveniently leave out the part about blood rushing up to her sex, plumping her labial lips and swelling her clitoris. She'd have to try to forget that. It wasn't all just gravity at work....

"That isn't sweat, sir. I, um, spilled my water when I took a drink after the try out."

He actually giggled. Giggled!

"Is your water bottle invisible? Because I don't see it yet it seems to be spilling more and more on you all right in the same spot."

Why did she even bother trying to get out of saying it?

He was in control and she was out of her own control. His hand possessing her pussy was symbolic of the overall situation. He had her by the proverbial short hairs!

She just had to give in. Do what he wanted. Say what he wanted.

Also, somehow, what she wanted. Even just the idea she was about to totally humiliate herself for a man who wanted her humiliated somehow made her fire blaze no matter how wet she was. That pussy juice wasn't like water putting out a fire. More like gasoline. So was the humiliation.

"You're right, sir. It isn't water from my water bottle."

Parker sounded mock surprised/mystified, "Really? What is it then?"

"It's.... It's... pussy juice."

"Pussy juice? Where is it coming from?"

"From-- from my pussy, sir."

"Really? You must really *like* working out. Maybe if we hire you you'd like to work out for me every day. We could arrange that. If I'm busy maybe I'll have someone else work you out. Since you like it so much."

She knew he had to have a self-satisfied smirk on his face but she couldn't see him from her position. Damn this pervert! Damn herself as well!

That hand. Her pussy. It was like those two anatomical parts meeting was her whole world. Everything else faded in significance.

His hand kept rubbed her pussy through her clothing. He did it slowly and casually to a point where she began to wish he would do more.

He did not make her agree to let him work her out every day or allow others he chose to work her out. It was a relief because she knew right then she'd say pretty much anything he wanted her to say. Along with the relief was also disappointment that he did not make her compromise herself and promise what she should not promise. She'd never felt relief and disappointment before in such a strong mix.

He kept his hand on her covered pussy but she felt him move around to stand between her spread legs.

"Tell me... Penny... if you were naked and if you were ordered to maintain this position... do you think you could hold it until the one who ordered you to do so achieved... satisfaction?"

"I would try, sir."

"You certainly seem like a strong candidate. Strong is probably not the most accurate term to use I guess. Not at all. Let's say you seem like you would be a most pleasing acquisition."

He moved his hand to the top of her covered slit and pressed down on her clitoral hood. She felt his pelvis move into docking position with her covered pussy. He ground lightly on her.

God help her! She wanted him to do it harder! She wanted to be naked and him naked, too. And in this same position! Fucking! Being fucked! By this pervert asshole!

Utterly impossible and utterly true.

"Is it fair to say you would do anything to please me and those I tell you to please?"

"Yes, sir."

"Is it fair to say you would be grateful for the opportunity to please me and mine?"

"Yes. Sir." She felt like she'd just handed her soul over to him.

"I will give you the opportunity to prove that. Right now. Why wait, right?"

Parker backed away and she wished he hadn't. The mix of what she felt now was much less relief and a lot more disappointment.

"You can stand now."

It was difficult for Penny to get out of that bent backwards position. She actually had to roll sideways down on the floor and rise up from that position. By time she did, dizzy, disoriented by lust as well, Parker was back sitting behind the desk with his feet crossed on top of the desk. He held that damn smart phone again looking over it at her. How could he look so casually at her after feeling her up? How could he look at her at all?

He seemed relaxed. Like he did this sort of thing all the time.

That couldn't be, right? He must have just found her overwhelmingly attractive, lost control of his normal demeanor, and just went for broke. Because she was special to him. At least physically. Some sort of sexual type for him.

He couldn't treat other cheerleader candidates or other women this way. He could never get away with it with anyone else, right? Lynn popped into her head. Well, yes, he could certainly get away with this behavior with Lynn. Heck, Lynn would like it. The thought had scorn attached to it until she suddenly realized her hypocrisy. She liked it, too, so far!

"I know you want to show how much you want to please and how you're willing to do anything. Trust but verify I always say."

She felt herself hold her breath. What was it going to be?

She knew it was going to be something absolutely awful.

Totally terrible.

Humiliating.

She could feel it. Whatever it was she was going to do it. Not even to maintain a pretense. Because her pussy would make her do it.

"So while I do some social networking on my phone just go ahead and clean my shoes."

She was at a loss. Clean his shoes? Like shoe shine them? She looked at his desktop for any washcloth or cleaning fluid.

Her clueless state must have been obvious to him, "With your mouth, Penny.

With your fucking slut mouth! I want them sparkling and free of any and all specks of dirt."

She was just so into her role. She was so committed. There was no turning back. That's what she told herself right then and what she would tell herself again and again later on. After.

She even succeeded in not showing any hesitation at all. That was really embracing the role. She bent at the waist and tipped her face forward like one of those drinking bird toys that dipped it's beak in and then back up from a glass of water, again and again.

Except once her mouth made contact with Parker's leather shoes her own "beak" stayed down there for a long time.

She started at the toe tip. It seemed a logical way to fulfill this completely illogical act.

Minutes passed as she worked her mouth across the top and sides of the first shoe. She wouldn't go near the sole of the shoe. A girl had to have standards and limits in anything she did! Besides, she was sure Mr. Parker never intended her to lick the sole of his shoes. No one would do that. It would be asking far too much.

She mostly avoided even looking at Mr. Parker. It was way too embarrassing. But, when she did, usually he was staring into his smart phone which he held between him and her. She wondered what was so fucking fascinating on that smart phone. Here she was basically going down on his shoes and she couldn't even hold his interest!

What she was doing did hold her pussy's interest however. She felt sopping wet. Somehow this was arousing her as much or even more than his hand on her pussy. She could barely keep herself from moving a hand down there to finger herself. No. No way. She could *not* just go and masturbate in front of this jerk.

He'd think these awful things he was making her do was turning her on. Which they were. But she was determined not to let him know that.

Contrary to that thought she licked the shoe leather with long unhesitating sweeps of her tongue and even moaned a little sometimes. She knew that communicated all he'd want to know about what was going on in her head. Her own little moans were confessing her perversion. She was betraying herself but she couldn't stop.

So why shouldn't she just move a hand down to her pussy? Why not?

The real reason. He hadn't told her to do it. Not yet at least. If he did she would. Until then... it would be improper... it would disrespect his command of her.

His words broke into her dedicated tonguing of his leathery shoes, "Don't just lick, shoe slut. Kiss them all over. Suck on them. I want fucking hickeys on my shoes!"

Oh! She hadn't realized!

She gave the instep some soft wet lip-crushing smooches, then treated the toe tip like a cock head. Not the way she had the rare times she gave head to a guy. No, it was like what she'd seen porn starlets do in porn videos. Like they were hungry for it. Starving for it. Loved it. Which, right now, was exactly how she herself felt.

Then she sucked hard on the tip. She made a vacuum with her mouth and sucked powerfully. She could really taste the shoe polish. She sucked the polish out of the leather pores.

She realized it probably wasn't considered edible or good for humans.

Fuck it. She sucked harder, her cheeks caved in, and a groan rattled in her throat.

She was so wet. Her pussy was so needy. She felt her hips swiveling, her pussy grinding backwards into air. She needed an orgasm. A cock. Something. Anything. She'd do anything he asked. Anything.

"Shoe slut, don't forget the underside. The part that hits the ground is always the dirtiest. That's the most important part to clean completely. Get to it, shoe slut."

Shoe slut? Damn him. It was true she guessed.

This time she did hesitate just a fraction of second.

Something was nagging at the corner of her mind. Something about the bottom of his shoes.

Oh, yeah. Hadn't she just been telling herself she wouldn't do that? That kind of thing? That she had some kind of standards?

Yes. She had.

Fuck it. Fuck that.

She thought her mental "Fuck that" was in answer to doing as he requested. But she found her mouth licking and sucking at the dirty sole of one leather shoe so obviously it meant her mental "Fuck that" referred to her own reservations about the act. A rejection by her of her own do not cross line she'd set minutes before.

She realized her moral compass was more like a moral weathervane swiveling in whatever direction the wind blew. And the wind was Parker. And he was a gale force wind.

The shoes weren't *that* dirty. Her tongue did catch some grains of grit. She didn't dare spit them to the side so she just swallowed them down. Didn't birds swallow grit on purpose to help with their digestion? It made her think of how she was still bent over at the waist like one of those drinking bird toys stuck in the forward position.

Mr. Parker didn't seem to think she was quite humiliated enough, "Find any gum down there? I may have stepped on some out in the parking lot. If it's there, be sure to get it."

There was no gum... but Mr. Parker was such an asshole! And... and... a freak!

Penny's squishy pussy tensed with reaction to the humiliation. It felt so good. Unearthly good.

He kept looking at the phone and it was always directly between her and his face. It was hard to see him anyway with his shoes in the way. They glistened with her saliva. She swept her tongue up and down and all around. She was determined to do a good thorough job. Whatever you do you may as well do it your best.

She worked away at the shoe bottoms but, at one point, she saw her saliva on the instep of the right shoe was dry and the leather was no longer shiny. For some reason that bothered her so she moved to lick more saliva onto it.

It surprised her that it pissed off Mr. Parker since she thought she was being quite dutiful. But he did have a logic for his anger even if it was twisted and humiliating.

"Shoe slut! You idiot! The bottom of the shoe is the dirtiest. That's why a good shoe slut always, and I mean always, cleans the top and sides first and the bottom last and never, and I mean never, moves her dirty filthy slutty shoe slut mouth from the sole back up to the sides or top. You're supposed to fucking clean it, not make it more dirty with your dirty mouth."

Penny expected this must be too much, he'd pushed her too far, so now she would actually stand up and then figuratively stand up for herself. But that wasn't the case. She just quickly moved her mouth... her dirty mouth... back to lick at the underside of his shoe.

She didn't even question how he called her an idiot and scolded her. She did wonder what she'd been thinking putting her filthy mouth on the supple leather of his shoe tops. She should have known better.

The way he treated her, his harsh words, only made her wetter and hotter. She could barely stand it.

If he handed her, well, anything, anything at all, and told her to shove it in her pussy she sure would have. Dildo. Cucumber. A thick stick. A fucking log! She would have crammed it inside her and would have been grateful for it. She felt so not-enough that it seemed nothing could be too-big.

She could barely believe herself when she applied suction to the sole of the shoe. Then moved her mouth to apply suction to another mouth-sized section of sole. Again and again. Really trying to get them as clean as possible. She could only get them just so clean though because she was using her dirty mouth.

Could he even see and appreciate what she was doing?

Without notice he pressed the freshly cleaned sole of his shoe flat up against her face. The toe was in her hairline and the rounded heel pressed sharply on her chin. He pushed firmly and her face rocked backward.

"That's sufficient for now. With my shoes freshly mouth polished we both know you understand your role."

She straightened. Her back hurt a little but her pride was mortally wounded. Her face felt steamy wet and she knew she was flushed from embarrassment and arousal.

He kept his feet on the desk and the smart phone held in front of him. He looked at her expectantly and his free hand made a rolling motion with one finger sticking out, like telling her to get on with it.

She did not know what he wanted from her.

He looked slightly irritated and a little amused as well, "I just let you clean my shoes. Quite a privilege for a shoe slut like you. Mind your manners and thank me."

"Thank you?"

"You're welcome. I'll let you do it again sometime since you show such proficiency."

When could she take off her clothes and get fucked by him? That's all she really wanted to know at that instant.

He made that rolling motion with his free hand again, "That's all. I've got things to do. Leave now."

Just... leave? But... that wasn't fair!

She came back to herself a little. What had she done? Why had she done it? She was disgusted by her actions, her obedience, the treatment she put up with, the taste in her mouth, and her overall arousal from it.

She turned to go.

"You are hired by the way. You have some useful potential that can be exploited." He really put the emphasis on the pronunciation of "exploited". Again with the innuendo. "Violet will call you and arrange further testing and training."

Penny wanted to say something, anything, to reclaim some shred of dignity. But she couldn't think of anything she could say that might do that even a little bit. She'd walked in here a luckless college-educated waitress hoping to better her situation and now she was about to leave having become some kind of shoe slut.

A very horny shoe slut!

Penny nodded her understanding to him and was about to leave but hesitated. She had nothing to say that could reclaim her dignity but it felt like something remained unsaid.

She glanced back at him sheepishly and saw he still held the smart phone pointed towards her, "Thank you. Sir."

She felt a rush of humiliating lust. She could not reduce the loss of dignity but she had been able to increase it!

Then she left. She really needed to get home and masturbate as long and as much as possible.

Penny drove home in her shitty decade-plus old hatchback with ceiling upholstery she'd had to staple back into place with an actual popped open stapler like it was a tiny nail gun.

For the whole twenty minute drive she thought of almost nothing other than what she'd just done. She nearly got in an accident at one point.

It would have been perhaps the first death by humiliation. If you didn't include suicides of course. But how many people ever died accidentally by humiliation?

She entered the red light somehow thinking it was green, then just in time, perceived the truck coming to T-bone her which would have cracked her hatchback like a hatchback-shaped egg. She'd instinctively slammed on the gas and shot ahead of the vehicular execution by inches. The short length of the two-door hatchback also saved her. If her vehicle was any less short she would been struck and spun even with the increase in speed.

She had no time for actual death. She was interested in the "little death" as the French – or someone French – supposedly called orgasms. She had to get home and get a little death going. And then another. As many as she could before she wore out. A real massacre if she could manage it.

She got into her apartment and pressed her back against the closed door like she'd been pursued. Perhaps by her lost dignity.

She looked down and saw the row of shoes and boots lined up against the wall. She and Lynn always took off their footwear on entry. Like it wasn't actually a piece of shit apartment with already worn and scored wood floors.

Looking at the shoes and boots reminded her of what she'd done for Mr. Parker. For him? What she'd done because he ordered her! Or told her. Whatever. She'd done it. That evil nerd shrimp bastard.

The memory replayed in her head and it felt like a punch to the tummy.

She looked at hers and Lynn's footwear lined up and saw some needed cleaning. Some had dirt. They could really use the services of her mouth....

This was crazy! These thoughts were making her pussy clench and producing more wetness.

Penny rushed to her bedroom and whipped off her clothes. She should fucking burn them! No time for that. Her pussy demanded attention. Commanded attention.

She lay spreadeagled on her bed. She was relieved Lynn wasn't home. Her fingers felt like miracle workers. Little magic wands made of flesh and bone.

She came in less than a minute. It did not satisfy her lust. It just poured fire on it.

Too external. She wanted penetration.

She went back to work on her pussy. This time with several fingers teaming up to act like a very short cock pushing in and out.

It took a few minutes this time to come. She still wasn't satisfied. She lay there, sweaty and damp, legs spread. She needed something. Something more.

She wondered if Lynn had a dildo or vibrator somewhere. Well, she definitely did. Penny had no doubt of it based on Lynn's personality. So sexually... willing.

Would Lynn have licked Mr. Parker's shoes? She probably already had! No way was Mr. Parker just waiting for the day Penny would show up. She wasn't even that type! She hadn't even known the type of "shoe slut" existed.

The thought of a dildo right then was very tempting but the idea of using Lynn's without permission... one that had already been inside her roommate... was not tempting at all.

Oh. So she did still have some standards!

She hated the pornographic stereotype but wondered if there was a cucumber in the fridge.

Would she really use one on herself? She would never know. At least not until their next shopping trip to the grocery store. She remembered that, as usual, the fridge was rather barren.

She'd use the handle of her own hairbrush. She went and got it from the bathroom. Nice and thick and long enough.

It was long enough but just fucking herself with it didn't seem like enough.

Suddenly she had an idea. It was horrible. Terrible. An embarrassment. Totally wrong.

And exactly perfect. Exactly what she needed.

Penny dashed naked over to the front door hoping Lynn wouldn't happen to come home right then. She grabbed one of her out-on-the-town little leather fancy boots she'd never yet found cause to actually wear.

Penny ran back to her bedroom, her uncovered too-big breasts jouncing and flopping heavily, some pussy juice leaking down her leg. She slammed her bedroom door and did an artless spinning back roll onto the bed like an Olympic pole vaulter going over the cross bar. Boot in one hand, hairbrush in the other.

She could hardly believe what she was about to do and couldn't bear to think about it. She also couldn't bear not to do it. She just... had to.

It felt like her only hope of getting satisfaction. No matter how weird.

Without any warming up – she already was warmed up – she moved the hairbrush handle end against her labial lips, pushing the lips to the side as she wiggled it into the entrance to her vagina.

She did not push.

Not yet. Not quite yet.

She used her left hand to bring her boot up to her face. She smelled it. Then she stuck its toe tip into her mouth and lovingly sucked at it.

Now. Now she was ready. Now it would be perfect.

Penny jammed the hairbrush into her pussy as far and as hard as she could. Successfully. The sides of the bristles rammed into the top of her slit supplying extra unexpected sensation to her clitoris.

She made a loud air-sucking gasp.

She was even more surprised when her orgasm hit just that quickly.

It was a loud thrashing orgasm that just kept going on. She jammed that hairbrush harder and harder and didn't give a damn if she injured herself. She didn't even try to thrust it in and out. It was just one long hard pussy stabbing via blunt object. Her bouncing worked her body to the edge of the bed and she nearly fell off by the time the orgasm died down.

Pulling the boot tip out of her mouth was difficult as her teeth were clenched with orgasmic reaction.

When she got the boot free she saw with dismay that there was a set of tooth imprints in the leather....

Now she really wouldn't ever wear her boots out on the town.

Lynn seemed a little surprised when Penny told her she was accepted to the cheerleader team. Surprised but then maybe a little excited too.

"I thought you could do it! Did it work? Did you act like me?"

Penny couldn't help but blush. She had to wonder what Lynn knew or would suspect. Whether or not Mr. Parker had treated her the same. "Oh, I just focused on doing my best and just ignored everything else."

Lynn tilted her head like she was trying to figure out exactly what that meant.

Penny nervously went on. She didn't usually have diarrhea of the mouth but she felt a real loss of confidence. "We'll see how it works out. If I fit in or not. I guess Violet is going to call and arrange for training."

Lynn raised her blonde eyebrows, "Violet the Violent. Yeah. She trained me, too. Stick with it and it will get better."

"What does that mean?"

"She's pretty rough. Almost like a guy with tits. She's very hard to please. Don't mouth off. She'll crush you if you do. Just do what she says as quickly and as well as you can."

"Well, I was sort of dreading it but now I'm really dreading it."

"I know what you mean. Trust me. After a while you'll look forward to seeing her and being seen by her."

"What does that mean?"

"You'll see."

Lynn maintained that aura of mystery around Violet and her training for the next couple days and wouldn't give any details at all. Penny didn't like being judged by a trainer like Violet or anyone. Or trained to be one rung above a stripper. But she was in good shape and cheer-leading was basically just coordinated team exercise. She could manage that easily.

That ordeal with Mr. Parker! She felt like her disgrace with Mr. Parker earned her hire. She wasn't going to let that go to waste. It could not be for nothing!

Obviously Violet's training would be much easier.

But she was wrong.

The next day in the late afternoon she was back at the stadium to work with Violet. Lynn was covering for her at Mack's until she got done. She'd grab a shower after and get over there then.

Lynn startled her when she left by saying she would give Esteban a blow job and pretend to be her, Penny, since it was her shift. She said Esteban would love that. She said it with a little smile so maybe she was kidding and maybe she wasn't. What was wrong with that girl?

Penny just gave her a troubled look.

Lynn noticed that look and told her, "If you think that's slutty just wait until Violet has you in all sorts of slutty positions at the stadium."

Penny left without comment not trusting herself to stay civil. Sure, Violet would have her bend and twist and jump or whatever. There certainly were some awkward, perhaps even slutty, positions during the try out. But that was one fuck of a long way from being any species of slutty similar to giving a blow job in a restaurant back room to a much older creepy married supervisor like Esteban. He treated the waitresses like sheep and Lynn giving in to him probably made it worse for everyone else.

She wore her best and newest leggings, tank top, and sports bra though Violet told her it didn't matter what she wore.

As if. How would Violet react if she showed up in a dress or wearing jeans?

Obviously it mattered.

Except, no, turned out it didn't.

They were in a small room with a well-polished wood floor and mirrors and it was just the two of them. Being alone with a woman who was there to judge her, one who was used to literally fighting other women, and knowing that if they ever did fight this woman would kick her ass, was intimidating.

"The reason I told you it does not matter what you wear is because you will now remove all your clothes."

"Uh. What?"

"I think I was clear. If you cannot be more eloquent you should keep your mouth closed until it can be put to a worthy task."

What did that mean? Had Mr. Parker said something to Violet about the shoe licking? Or did she just generally know that was his thing and that was what it took to make the team? Or did it mean something else, something more imminent?

Her clothes. Big deal she guessed. Everyone was naked under their clothes anyway, right? Just two women here, right?

Penny knew she was fooling herself a little bit. She remembered how Violet had looked at her and the other women trying out the other day. A hungry sexual look.

Getting naked in front of Violet was really pretty much the same as getting naked in front of a man. She mentally sighed. In for a penny, in for a pound. She usually avoided that saying due to the name play. She kind of hated it but it fit this occasion.

She was not going to throw away her sacrificed dignity from her encounter with Mr. Parker. That had to be for something!

She took off her clothes.

Violet didn't even pretend to look away.

Didn't even pretend not to be a lesbian either! She actually licked her lips several times while looking over more and more of Penny's revealed body.

Once she was nude but feeling naked – the lack of clothes made her nude but Violet's lascivious looks made her feel naked – Violet put her through an exhausting regime.

Penny was self-conscious at first running in place, jumping, and balancing. But you could get used to anything and once she became winded she had to concentrate on the physical tasks without worry of what Violet was looking at or imagining she'd do to the parts she looked at.

Eventually, after half an hour of physical activity, she found herself doing the splits by order of Violet. With no clothes on! He pussy just inches from touching the wood floor!

"Hold that position." Violet kept a commanding and confident tone that assumed obedience. Correctly so far with Penny.

Penny wondered, not for the first time, why she was putting herself through all this.

It was humiliating but she tried to be philosophical about that. It was really only Mr. Parker and now Violet and she didn't care what they thought anyway. Right? So, who cares? No one else would know and they seemed like they were used to slutty obedience so she wouldn't really even stand out to them would she?

Penny realized suddenly that Violet was in her personal space. Up to this point she'd stood ten feet away like a Marine at attention while barking her orders. But now she was right there squatted down next to her.

Touching distance.

"What's this?" Violet tugged on Penny's dark pubic hair, pulling on a twist of it just above her clitoral hood!

Penny opened her mouth to angrily protest the indiscretion but all that came out were stammers and indecipherable syllables.

"Talking is not the strong suit of sluts. I see you must be one just like the others. That's good though. We value sluts around here. I know what this is anyway obviously. Pubic hair. Your bush. Are you from the 60s? Come her in a time travel machine?"

Penny's stammers dwindled into silence.

"Shave this bird's nest. You won't be able to do it proper since it's obvious you haven't done it before. Tell Lynn I said she has to shave it and then you let her. I'll get a full report from Lynn and I'll be inspecting you in the future whenever I want. And believe me I will want."

Despite thinking that now things really couldn't get worse, they did. Penny felt Violet release her small gather of pubic hairs and drift her hand down to trace her fingers up and down Penny's slit which was spread and particularly vulnerable due to her maintained splits position.

Her pussy was also particularly vulnerable because of it being rather wet. When had that happened? Penny tried to figure it out, dedicating some of the precious remaining brain cells that were still firing to solving that mystery even as Violet easily slid two big fingers up her pussy. And then in and out repeatedly.

The mystery of the wet pussy became the mystery of the soaking wet pussy.

Was it because her pussy was still revved up from what she'd done for Mr. Parker and then coming back to the scene of the incident?

Or was it being naked for half an hour with Violet's eyes fondling her?

Or was it from following all those commands to assume humiliating positions?

Or the idea of having to ask Lynn to shave her pussy?

All of the above?

Penny didn't know what to do. Violet was totally taking advantage and, even though it shouldn't, it felt good. Damn her. "Her" being both Violet and herself.

Blood rushed to Penny's already swollen labial lips and she felt a little dizzy.

Violet reached out helpfully and grabbed Penny's bare right breast, steadying her and squeezing the big breast.

"Your tits are so big I would have thought they were fakers. But they're so soft. All real, huh?"

"Yes. They're real." Funny how Penny could assemble the needed words when Violet wanted her to say something but not when she herself had something to say.

"What about your sexy lips. The ones on your mouth. They are so full and sexy. Natural or augmented?"

"Natural. Real."

"Best of both worlds then. You look enhanced but are not enhanced. You were built to be the slut you are."

Penny wanted to angrily correct her assumption that she was some kind of slut. But that would not further her ends and she doubted Violet would be open to debate even as her long fingers went further up Penny's wet pussy with each thrust.

Penny doubted she had any credibility in the I'm-not-a-slut department.

Violet pulled and tweaked at Penny's swollen right nipple, jammed her fingers up Penny's spread pussy, and rotated a thumb pad over her clitoris, popping it out of its hood and working it rapidly.

Penny realized she was going to orgasm. Like this!

"Oh God!"

Just a moment before the orgasm spilled Violet abruptly pulled both hands away and stood up. Penny couldn't stop herself and she fell onto her side.

No orgasm!

She needed it!

Should she just give it to herself in front of Violet?

"Who's working for who, slut? Why should you get an orgasm when you've done nothing for me?"

"I... I don't know. Please."

"Please is polite but you can be even more polite. What do you think you should call me?"

"Violet?"

"Put a 'Mistress' in front of that and you're onto something. Maybe even onto my big dildo."

Mistress? Did she say Mistress? Wasn't that some kind of BDSM thing?

And... dildo? Violet wanted to fuck her? Penny guessed she shouldn't be that surprised. She knew Violet was a lesbian and she knew she herself was hot so it was pretty much just common sense. Still....

Penny felt a powerful need in her pussy to do whatever needed to be done. This orgasm denial was a bitch! Because of that selfish bitch Violet!

"Please, Mistress."

"I'm not sure a slut like you is worth my time though. I'm in it for the long haul. I'm not the get them off and let them leave type. Do you promise to obey me always, immediately, in all things, no matter what?"

"Um, sure."

"What the fuck did you just say?"

"I meant yes, Mistress. I promise."

"Fine. You better not be a liar."

Penny knew she wasn't a liar. Not in general and not usually. But, of course, she had just now lied. She couldn't just run around obeying this amazon lesbian in *all* things from now on. No way! But she needed that orgasm right now. Yes way!

Violet pushed a cheap swivel office chair over next to Penny. She pulled off her own clothing from the waist down, sat in the chair, and spread her legs. She did not seem at all self-conscious.

"Since you're being polite I'll give you the privilege of licking my pussy. The better you do at it the more often I'll let you do it."

Penny didn't think that sort of motivation would work with her. She didn't want to do it this time let alone more times in the future. Going down on this amazon on a regular basis? No thanks.

Even though she marveled that she was going to do this now she knew she had to. She felt like she physically needed to do it. Her pussy made demands and was at least as demanding as the demanding Violet.

She awkwardly got out of the splits position. Even though Violet was right there she started to stand up.

"Don't bother standing. Just submarine on over here and bring your torpedo tits."

"Um. What?" Penny felt stupid. Literally. She was having a hard time thinking. Even just understanding words and putting things together. She didn't think her pussy had enough brain cells to be running her like this.

"I mean fucking crawl, bazooka tits. I like a slut to crawl as often as possible. It's a natural state for you sluts. Standing on two legs is like a dog standing on two legs. Sure, you can do it, but it doesn't look natural. Not to me."

Penny sunk back down to her knees and then put her hands forward and her weight onto them. She was very conscious of her heavy breasts swinging to and fro beneath her. They felt heavier than usual, swollen with arousal.

Violet was also aware of Penny's lovely out-sized breasts, "Look at those milk jug boobs flopping against each other. Those are your two best features. Make sure to swing them back and forth as you crawl over here. Sometime soon you'll be doing that for our investors."

Penny didn't like this talk of "investors" but obviously Violet was wrong about anything like that so she could just ignore it and focus on what was important: please Mistress Violet and be allowed to orgasm.

Penny, possessed by a sense of unreality, crawled into place between Violet's muscular legs and moved her face close in to Violet's pussy. She couldn't help but note Violet had a big bush of pubic hair. What a hypocrite!

She couldn't let that awareness stop her from doing whatever she had to do to get her orgasm. She used her nose like a cowcatcher in front of an Old West train to move the pubic hair to the side and give her mouth access. Just as Penny's mouth made contact with Violet's pussy, Violet spoke to her.

"There you go, Mongo Tits. Drink from my pussy. Please your Mistress. There is nothing more important to you now than pleasing me."

Was Violet trying to brainwash her or something? It wouldn't work!

Penny's tongue licked and then pushed inside Violet's pussy. Mistress Violet's pussy.

Penny was oddly gratified that Mistress Violet's pussy was already quite wet. That proved she was turned on. That Penny had turned her on. Violet had enjoyed watching Penny's nude body and strained positions. Enjoyed bossing her around and humiliating her.

Well... good for her. Good for them both.

Mistress Violet's pussy did not have a strong taste but the subtle taste was somehow awesome to Penny.

After a minute of oral work Violet gently cuffed her on the head, "Stop pussyfooting around my pussy. Get your face in there all the way. Get your plump lips inside my pussy lips. Work that pussy for your new Mistress."

Penny just did as ordered. She didn't feel like Violet, or her own pussy, gave her any choice in the matter.

She also found... she wanted to. She wanted to do what Violet said and she also wanted to do *whatever* Violet said.

Her own pussy was dripping with need. She wanted to masturbate herself. Right there in front of Mistress Violet. Which felt doubly wrong. That was naughty and wicked by any previous standards she held and, also, Mistress Violet had told her not to so it was twice as wrong.

It was hard to breath with her lips inside Mistress Violet's pussy. She sucked in air through her nose which was planted against Mistress Violet's clitoral hood and the tuft of pubic hair there. The strong feminine smell of Mistress Violet was intoxicating and overwhelming.

As she licked and tongue thrust she felt light-headed. Like she might pass out.

"You big tits slut! You fucking did it!" Violet grabbed at Penny's head with both hands and ground her face into Violet's clenching pussy. Mistress Violet was coming!

Things started to go black for Penny. She couldn't breath! She was going to die this way!

Moments later Violet released her. More like pushed her away and she toppled sideways.

She was alive! No big death for her. But would she get the "little death" of an orgasm?

"Get on your hands and knees, Balloon Tits."

Exhausted from air deprivation but eager, Penny did as ordered wondering what was coming. Hopefully herself!

She saw Mistress Violet held a medium-sized red dildo, just a cylinder, not at all an anatomically correct imitation of a penis. Penny figured maybe Violet didn't want anything that even looked like a real cock involved in her lesbian play.

Penny was surprised when standing Violet straddled her while Penny was on hands and knees. Violet faced towards Penny's rear!

Penny was even more surprised when bare-bottomed Violet sat down on her while still facing towards her ass.

Penny welcomed the dildo when it thrust into her. Welcomed it with hot pussy juice and a flexing pussy sheathing it.

Violet's weight was quite a burden but the dildo was a blessing. It made it worth it. It made everything worth it.

"Take a "step" with one hand or knee."

Penny did as ordered and immediately Violet pulled the dildo almost free and then slammed it back home into Penny's pussy.

"Take another step."

Penny moved her right knee forward and again Violet pulled the dildo almost free and than slammed it back in. Penny grunted a welcome back to it.

"You see how this works now, slut? Each step you take I pump you one. The faster you walk the faster I fuck your pussy. Go ahead, walk at will, I'll enjoy the ride up here. You're my big girl version of "My Little Pony"."

Penny did see how it worked. She felt it as well as she bore Violet's weight and walked forward on knees and hands and the dildo thrust in and out. She "walked" faster and faster. Even though she began out of breath and became even more out of breath she kept going as fast as she could.

The room was fairly small so she had to keep turning. Once she ran head first into a wall and a couple times she ran into a wall with her side and hip. It was hard to pay attention to obstacles, suck in enough air, and enjoy the fucking all at the same time.

She had some remaining self-awareness apart from herself. At one point, light-headed, she felt like she was floating over the scene watching herself be ridden reverse cowgirl style by Violet. All covered in perspiration, wetness on her inner thighs, redness on her scraped knees, her red and needy pussy clinging at that sliding dildo.

It was humiliating. What if anyone came in and saw what they were doing? She was embarrassed for herself.

It was also undeniably hot. Not just the sensation of that slick smooth cylinder working in and out of her depths. The humiliation itself was an extreme turn on. Doing something totally new to her and totally naughty was exciting.

She knew she'd regret all this. Just knew it. How couldn't she? But she was also somehow glad it was happening. At least at the moment. It was like finding new sections of her sexual personality. Like finding new rooms in a house you've lived in all your life.

"Come on, Slut Pony! Gallup! Gallup for your orgasm! Giddy-up girl!"

Penny eagerly did as Mistress Violet ordered. She put on a burst of painful knee-slamming speed, careened off a wall, then another, and then collapsed under Violet from a blend of sheer exhaustion, Violet's weight, and a body-rippling orgasm.

Violet stood up off her, pulled out the dildo, and then wiped it in Penny's hair.

"That was a good work out. Come here at two tomorrow and we'll do it again. More or less. Well, more. I took it light on you this time."

This was light?

"Make sure your slut roomie shaves your pussy. No more pubic hair for you. If I see a hair down there in the future I'll spank you. Well, I'll spank you either way but much harder if you have any pubic hair."

Barely able to speak, Penny still couldn't help herself, "Spank me? You're joking!"

Wham! The resounding impact on her rear and the wave of pain prematurely ended the enjoyment of the aftereffects of her orgasm.

"They don't call me Violet the Violent for nothing. And you better make calling me Mistress Violet your everything."

Penny's reply was instinctive and automatic, "Sorry, Mistress Violet."

Why had she apologized? It should be the other way around!

"Know what else, Pony Slut? Besides spanking you, I will rip out, by hand, any pubic hairs I find on that pussy of yours that now belongs to me. What once was yours now is mine. For instance, your pussy used to be yours and now it belongs to me."

Penny's reply was instinctive and automatic, "I understand, Mistress Violet."

"And I understand you. You're a stupid slut. Stupid sluts make stupid slut mistakes. See. I'm very understanding. I understand that when you make those stupid slut mistakes I need to spank the snot out of you."

"Now get dressed and get out of here. See you tomorrow. Fuck you tomorrow."

Penny got dressed.

Penny went home.

She alternately floated on sexual satisfaction and sunk with dismay. Her emotions bounced around like a bobber with a fish on the line.

In one way she had been successful. She had acted just like Lynn. Just like a dumb submissive.

Exactly like one.

Penny went back to her apartment for a quick shower and a bite to eat before going to Mack's to tag off with Lynn.

During her shower she looked down at her pussy. Fucking traitor.

She looked at her pubic hair. Shave it? Really? She wouldn't do it. Why would she? Because Violet said so? That was hardly a reason to alter her personal private grooming.

But it wasn't really Violet who wanted it. It was Mistress Violet. Now...that.... That seemed like a perfectly reasonable reason to do it.

But... if she did it... wasn't that an admission, an expectation, that she'd let Violet view – or more than view – her pussy in the future? It was. Based on her words Violet, Mistress Violet, expected to be doing more of the same as today or maybe even worse.

Or better. Depending on how one looked at it....

Deciding whether or not to shave it was pretty much the same as deciding if she would let Violet violate her again. Violet the Violent violator!

She had to hold off the decision anyway as Violet had made it clear she was not to do it herself. She was going to have to ask Lynn to do it. Obviously that was another reason to not do it. How could she ever ask Lynn to do it? She figured Violet made a big mistake by requiring that. It made it much less likely she'd become some kind of... submissive... to the demanding lesbian.

Too bad for her!

There was no helping it. Penny vigorously masturbated in the shower. She worked her pussy like she was mad at it. Which she sort of was.

The orgasm was a pleasure and a relief. But it could not hold a candle – or a dildo – to the orgasm Mistress Violet had given/forced on her.

Penny thought about searching for and using Lynn's dildo or vibrator, whatever she had. But she realized it wasn't the dildo that made the power level of her orgasm with Mistress Violet so wonderful. It was all those other things. The commands, her obedience, the risk, the pain, the humiliation, the taboo lesbian acts, the name-calling. All that. Everything else in and around and on top of the sex.

She couldn't get that from a dildo. So far she only knew of two people who could give her these foreign forbidden elements. Mistress Violet and Mr. Parker.

Damn them!

She ate a turkey sandwich, half of it in her hatchback on the way to Mack's. In the cramped break room hanging up her purse, Lynn came in like she'd been watching for her. Probably had, probably wanted to get home.

"Penny!" Lynn said enthusiastically.

"Lynn!" Penny said with faked enthusiasm.

"How'd it go with Violet?"

"Um. Good. I guess."

"Did she get you into lots of weird positions?"

"I guess. Yeah. A little."

Lynn brought her face close to Penny, uncomfortably close, and tilted her head to one side, "Did she make you come?"

"Lynn!"

"Come on. Did she dig up your hidden submissive lesbian side?"

"Damn, Lynn! I'm... I'm not... some sort of... what... why are you asking things like that?"

"Hey, calm down. She did the same stuff with me. It's awful and kind of great, too, isn't it?"

"How did you... I mean... why didn't you... I don't want to talk about it. I mean... there's nothing to talk about."

"Mistress Violet told me. Well, texted me. Don't even try to lie. She even sent a photo. Of course, I would have believed her anyway. She doesn't lie to people like us. If she even considers us "people". I mean, she can lie but lying to a slut like you or me she would consider beneath her."

"Don't be calling us sluts. At least not me!"

"Well, we are, aren't we? A slut is controlled and led by her pussy. That's pretty much us, isn't it?"

"No. No, it's not."

"If you saw the photo Mistress Violet sent of you I doubt you'd bother with the denying."

"What did it... show?"

"I'll just say it gives me a good idea what to get you for Christmas."

"Please don't think of me that way."

"Can't be helped now. Besides, I already thought it. That's why I encouraged you to try out. I thought you'd like it if you gave it a chance or were forced to. You always act better-than-that and all that. Why don't you even have a boyfriend when you're so hot?"

"You think... it's because I'm a lesbian?"

"No. You don't have a girlfriend either, right? It's because you are really a submissive and you sense you can't be truly happy unless you give up all control and live to serve. But you can't stand that idea either. You reject it without giving it a chance because you were raised to be independent."

"Well... what's wrong with that?"

"Nothing if you're that type. But not everyone is and you aren't."

"I am that type! That's who I am."

"That's who you pretended to be you mean. But it wasn't the truth."

"You can't say that. You don't know me better than I know myself."

"Not me. I'm just another dumb slut. Like you. It's Mistress Violet who knows best."

"But... I'm not... that!"

"Photo she sent says different. Photo says a thousand words you know. Ha!

This one probably says more."

"Show me the photo." Penny didn't actually want to see it. She dreaded seeing it. But she wanted to be able to do damage control and she couldn't do as good a job if she didn't know what the photo showed. She hated the idea of a compromising photo of her being out there, maybe sent back and forth or, who knows, intercepted by persons unknown.

They could get the wrong idea about her. Just like Lynn already had!

Now Lynn used her teasing voice, "Oh, you don't remember all the slutty things you did? You were too busy obeying your Mistress to take notes? The power of the orgasms wiped your memory?"

"Fuck off, Lynn."

"Actually, fuck on. Mistress Violet says I need to perform a certain personal task for you."

Penny knew her face must have looked absolutely stricken to her roommate. The shaving of her pubic hair!

"I can tell by that look you know exactly what I'm talking about."

What could Penny say now? That Violet was making that up or had it wrong? She couldn't decide in time how to approach this.

"Penny, I normally always do whatever Mistress Violet says and I'm sure you're like that or soon will be, too. But I can do a good job of it or a shitty job. You know Violet the Violent didn't get that nickname for nothing. Errant pubic hairs on sluts seems to really piss her off."

Penny inwardly shrink down with dread. She couldn't give up this cheerleader opportunity. She already dreaded / looked forward to facing Violet again. But, an angry Violet the Violent? She didn't want that.

"Lynn... what is your point?" She tried to put an exasperated this-is-silly tone in her voice to at least pretend none of what Lynn suspected was anywhere near the truth.

"I've seen your looks. You've looked down on me and how I am even though, turns out, you're the same as me even if you don't admit it yet. So, I'll do a good job on your pussy if you prove to me and to yourself that you're the same as me."

"How could I even prove that?"

"Pretty easily. Easy as a slut. I tried to be you for Esteban today. I even wore your name tag. It wasn't good enough. He wasn't happy. I feel bad for him. So, no pretend, lets give him the real Penny. He's working all day and night again today so you have all shift. I know he's going to invite you to take a break with him. Just do whatever he wants."

"That's – that's so wrong, Lynn! He's married with kids! He's an asshole!"

"Do it. Guess what? I bet you end up loving it."

Penny tried a new direction, "Lynn, just... stop. You'd be jealous anyway."

"No. I won't be. Sluts like you and me don't mind sharing. Know why? Because they share us. We get shared. It's what we do and what's done to us."

Penny just looked at Lynn. She felt betrayed. By Lynn for putting her up to this. By Violet for sending that photo to Lynn. Most of all, though, by herself. She should be slamming the door on this ridiculous demand. Instead she was just standing there staring at Lynn.

Lynn turned, got her purse, and left.

"You wanna extra break we can go hang out in my office."

There it was again. Esteban's insinuated invitation for sex at work.

But there was something different his time.

"Sure."

Esteban's neutral expression, well really, more like underlying angry expression, showed a moment of surprise. He hadn't expected Penny to agree.

That makes two of us, thought Penny.

He turned and she followed him to his office.

What am I doing, thought Penny. She actually didn't know. She was clueless what she'd do in that cramped little office of his. Not what he wanted. But then, why was she going there with him now when she'd always turned down his like-clockwork invitations with the same counter-clockwork recycled words?

He flopped down in his chair, "Close the door, Penny. Let's enjoy this break."

Penny could barely fit in the office which must have originally been intended as a closet. She awkwardly closed the door. She turned back to him.

Why did he look so smug?

"Your sexy little roomie showed me an interesting photo today. Very interesting."

Oh. That was why.

She hadn't even known Violet was taking any pictures and now both Lynn and Esteban had seen it and she still hadn't! Who knew how many others had seen it or would in the future....

"What photo?"

"I'm sure you can guess. It's for me to know the exact details. Up until you see the desktop background on my computer."

"You're kidding, right? You put it up on your computer screen?"

"Show me that body of yours you've been keeping from me."

"What?"

"Take off your clothes."

"But... we're at work..."

"We're taking a break. We can do what we want. We will."

"Someone could come back here."

"Don't care. No harm. They get a free show, good for them. Show me those chest puppies. Let them out to play."

It was weird. Just having come back here with him when she always refused and should have refused this time she felt committed. Like she was already obligated to do whatever he told her to do.

She even told herself she had to because he had a compromising photo of her. Of course, she couldn't be sure he really had it, or what it showed, or if he wouldn't still share it if she did as he asked. He hadn't even threatened to use it in any way.

She was too busy to figure all that out. Too busy taking off her clothes.

The moment she was entirely topless she felt a surprising thrill. Her "chest puppies" as he'd called them were swaying heavily back and forth with her movements getting her socks off in the crowded space. There was no use lying to herself. Her nipples were hard. She didn't know when that happened but they were hard as hard can be. Plus, her pussy was flooding.

Once down to her panties in front of creepy predatory Esteban she hesitated. It seemed like one last line to cross. Her pantie line? She was reluctant to cross it. It seemed like a one way trip. No jumping back across to the correct side.

She didn't know it then but she was wrong. It was by no means any sort of a final line. There were more lines to cross. Many more.

She hooked her fingers into the waist band of her panties and stopped. It wasn't so much not wanting to show her pussy to Esteban. It was more she did not want him to see how wet she was.

Esteban's dark eyes still looked angry but his tight twisted smile showed amusement.

He was fucking enjoying her reluctance!

Asshole!

That made up her mind. She'd show him. Literally.

She pushed down her panties and picked them up. They were darkened with wetness anyway. He must have known she was aroused even before her damp matted bush came into view.

She was at a loss what to do with her panties in her hand.

Esteban wasn't, "Just give those to me. I like to keep them. They come in handy."

She handed them over. Come in handy? What the fuck was he talking about? Did he jerk off in them or take them home to join some trophy collection? Gross or gross, either way.

Esteban unzipped his pants and pushed them down his legs. She saw his dark brown narrow cock spring up already hard.

"Today's a good day. About two hours ago your sexy buddy Lynn was right there where you are wearing what you're wearing. Nothing."

Well, she thought, that's nice, thanks for that. Her pussy was hot and she actually trembled in the warm little room. She felt a like a race horse a moment before the gate opens and the race starts.

"Don't worry, I'm going to give you something to wear. First, get down on your knees and show me how much you respect me. Show me how hungry you are for it."

It was pretty obvious what he was wanting from her!

Her reaction was the surprise. To her and probably to him. She got down on her bare knees on the cold cement floor and knee walked the few inches until her head hovered over his bare crotch.

That cement was so cold and her pussy was so hot!

She looked at his hard cock and felt the thrill of resignation. That cock was what she was here to do. She should just be grateful he only wanted a blow job and wasn't going to actually fuck her.

Her pussy totally disagreed though.

Just as she started to lean forward to put her mouth to work he put one palm against her forehead and held her in place, "Wait a sec, lucky Penny."

His hand left her head and she held still as she watched, dumbfounded, as he twisted around to reach a shelf behind him with her panties in his hand. When his hands came back he still held panties.

But not hers!

Hers were a lacy purple variation and these were a bright diaphanous yellow. They had an image of a cat's head on the crotch.

She knew those panties! She'd seen Lynn wear them from time to time since Lynn often liked to wander around the apartment in undies or less. Lynn once pointed at her crotch adorned with those panties and said, "See my pussy?" with a grin on her face.

So Esteban took Lynn's panties earlier. She guessed that should be expected of the creep. Just like he took her own panties. No surprise.

The surprise was what Esteban did with Lynn's "pussy" panties.

Esteban pulled them onto Penny's head, sliding their waistband downward until they reached her upper lip and she wore the panties almost like a low-slung hair net. From the smell she knew the front of the panties were faced forward which meant there was an upside down cat head image approximately covering her nose and between her eyebrows.

Penny didn't know why she just knelt there while he centered and adjusted it to his satisfaction. It was on her head. Too late now to do anything.

She still felt obligated by his expectations. By Lynn's expectations. By her own. He could do almost anything and she knew she'd just... let him. Let him do anything until he was finished. Whatever turned him on no matter how humiliating or twisted.

She suspected it would turn her on as much or more.

The panties had a very strong fresh feminine smell. The whole cat head image area was very damp. Esteban must have fondled Lynn while she wore them or had her finger herself while wearing them. Hadn't Lynn told her he liked to order the waitresses to do that sort of self-pleasuring in front of him?

How sick. How hot. It definitely turned her on more than it made her want to turn away.

The crotch-band was slim so she could still see Esteban's hard cock inches away. And her mouth wasn't covered. Of course Esteban wouldn't want her mouth limited in any way.

Esteban broke her out of her paralysis, "There, lucky Penny. You look just right. Go ahead. Do what you want to do with that sexy mouth of yours."

Penny leaned forward but was loath to actually go down on him. He hadn't quite ordered her. He'd told her to do what she wanted to do. Well, with her mouth. She should bite him!

She continued leaning forward and pressed her full lips against his cock, near the top. She licked. She could taste... something... on it.

As she licked and nuzzled he groaned. That made her feel good. All too good. Why was pleasing this creep so rewarding?

Her licks became more fervent and her nose kept bumping his cock. A clear fluid leaked out of the tip and slid down the cock like a dripping candle. It obscured the previous flavor. She figured that previous flavor must have been the flavor of Lynn's pussy. That or some other waitress's pussy. That disgusting thought just made her own flame rage hotter. Her pussy wax was running from her internal heat.

Her face and tongue kept bopping his cock making it bounce and dance. She wanted more of it. She wanted to do more for it. She captured the cock's head in her mouth. She engulfed the cock further by sliding her mouth down until the head jammed against the back of her mouth.

She barely restrained her gag reflex. That the flexing muscles in her mouth and throat from the near gags brought him pleasure became obvious by his deep groans of satisfaction.

She worked up and down in short motions. She couldn't deep throat. She'd never had success. Not that she ever tried very hard. Esteban's cock wasn't too big so, if she were going to try again, this would be a good one but she had no interest in that.

Not because of the choking discomfort or how some men might think a woman who did that was as slutty as a porn starlet. Esteban already thought she was a slut.

No, she was eager. Not to get it over with. She actually felt eager to make him come, eager to give him satisfaction, eager to taste his sperm. She knew she wasn't a slut no matter what Esteban, Lynn, Violet, Parker.... apparently everyone... seemed to think of her. But right now, these moments, she was a slut.

She wanted his come and she wanted nothing else other than that.

It was a strange dirty purity of intent.

With her mouth full and occupied it seemed Esteban felt it would be the perfect time to say things without fear of her interrupting him.

"This is by far the best use of your mouth Penny. Talking? Fuck that. No one wants to hear you talk back. God gave you a mouth like that, big sexy lips like that, you know even God wants you sucking as much cock and licking as much pussy as possible."

It should have made her angry but it just made her incredibly hot.

"You're good with your sucking and licking but you can get much better. I'm going to be your trainer. You'll have a lot of hard training on my hard cock. But all that hard work will be worth it. To me."

She felt gratified she was doing a good enough job that he wanted her to do this again but she also wasn't sure if she should again. He was married. He had all those other waitresses. Including her roommate! Plus, he was a creep.

"Every fucking shift, Penny. Come here ready to suck. Every shift. Shit, I'll give you more shifts. Work you every day. If my sack is empty then I'll let you suck off a dishwasher. You'll like that. You'll thank me."

No, she wouldn't! She would not suck off some lowly dishwasher and then thank him. She almost shook her head but realized she couldn't with his cock in her mouth.

Why was she focused on how she wouldn't thank him after giving a dishwasher a blow job at his command when she should be focused on how she wouldn't even do any such blow job?

She had to admit, though, it didn't seem that far-fetched that she'd go down on someone he told her to including a dishwasher. Not right then at that particular moment.

"Yes, you too-good-for-it know-it-all bitch. Every day. Suck my cock wearing someone's panties on your head. Sniffing their dried or not so dried juices. Maybe I'll let you choose sometime. I've got a nice selection in my collection. Not counting ex-waitresses, just your current co-workers, I've got Camilla, Ariana, Lisa, Gianna, Jade, and Andrea. Whose do you want to wear next?"

Why oh why did he have to talk to her in such a humiliating way?

Why oh why did it turn her on so much to be verbally shamed?

"You want Andrea's? The new girl? I had her on her second night. She's a decade younger than you but already a better cock sucker. Don't worry. I'll get you trained up. Me and Pablo and Juan the dishwashers.”

Faces popped into Penny's bobbing head. Andrea. Her sleek dark hair and young eager face. Apparently eager for cock, too. Just as eager as Penny now was. Pablo and Juan. Juan was quiet and not that bad looking though he was even shorter than Esteban. But Pablo. She felt a dirty dark shiver of eager fear. He was dark, fatty, and mean-looking. Although, she had to admit, he probably wouldn't be too mean once she had his dirty cock in her mouth. Not if she did a good enough job with it.

She knew the way she was thinking was all fucked up. All because she wanted to get fucked up. Up her pussy!

“I hear you like pussy now, too. Don't worry, I schedule extra staff so you can team up sometimes. Enough to take care of tables while others take care of me. Like that? You and maybe Lisa both going down on my cock and balls at the same time. Have you and whoever, Ariana let's say, put on a little show for me first.”

She didn't like him making all these bizarre plans involving her. Pretending like something like that would ever even happen. It was shameful and wrong and disrespectful, and oh so intriguing.

“With those extra shifts and with all the extra perks I give you, letting you suck me and Pablo and Juan off, you'll need to do your part. Nothing is free. You have to split your tips with me from now on. Only fair.”

What!?! No fucking way! She had just told Lynn a few days ago how crazy wrong that was. If she was sucking all those cocks she shouldn't be making less money, should she? Of course... if she made more money from it that would make her some kind of prostitute and she didn't want that either.

She almost shook her head again but stopped herself in time. She wasn't going to run around, or crawl around, and suck all those cocks. Not going to happen.

"I see you agree."

Why had he said that? Then she realized her mouth bobbing up and down on his cock made it look like she was nodding vigorous agreement. She should pull her mouth off him so she could verbally set him straight. But she hated to give up that meat lollipop even for a few seconds. She might miss the sperm eruption!

He pushed on her forehead again and, surprisingly, they had a brief contest with Penny trying to keep his cock in her mouth and Esteban trying to get her to give it up. He won and a thick strand of pre-cum laced saliva swung between her lower lip and his cock. He captured it with a finger and flung it into her hair.

"Nodding isn't good enough, Penny. I need to hear you agree to share half your tips with me."

She found her voice though speaking felt like a lost function only just barely recovered though it had only been mere minutes since she'd last used it. It was like trying to use a brand new third arm she'd just grown, "Esteban... my tips... are most of my pay. If I give half... to you. Then... I'll make a lot less... even if you work me every day."

"I know how your pay and tips work. It seems like you don't know how this works. I don't think I explained it all the way to you. Not only do you get to suck lots of cock and learn to become an expert cocksucker, you also get fucked sometimes. And, today, right now, and when you suck all these other cocks, we will let you finger your pussy and you will have permission to come."

She began to respond defiantly but then his words sunk in. Sticking some fingers up her pussy right then seemed crucially important. Getting to come. Maybe it was a privilege and not a right. Like driving?

"What? You want to just suck and suck cock after cock and you don't even get to come?"

No. She didn't want that. If she was sucking all that cock it was only fair she get to come. Damn him!

"Fine. Whatever." Her pussy welcomed her long-nailed fingers sliding in.

"Say it all the way, nice and clear. Promise me."

"All right. Esteban. I'll..." Was she really going to say it? She would find out the same time Esteban did. "Yes. I'll do it. You get half my tips. From now on. I promise"

"For Pablo and Juan, you'll give them extra smoke breaks and do dishes when they take breaks or whenever they tell you?"

Even out of her mind with lust and confusion she noted how he said "whenever they tell you" instead of "whenever they ask you". Plus, with how waitress pay went she'd only be making a little over two dollars an hour in pay anytime she was doing dishes and without any hope of tips.

"Yes. Yes. I'll do it. Whatever it takes. I'll do it. Whatever you say. Whatever they say."

She was ramming three fingers home, in and out, hard and abrupt, like she was punishing herself with pleasure. They were only part of the blended pleasure. She knew Esteban was watching and enjoying her spectacle and that raised her lust higher.

Giving in to him, though. That sick wrongness. That horrible commitment to do herself moral and financial harm in exchange for immediate short term pleasure that should be under her own control anyway. Somehow that made everything the best. The absolute best. There was nothing like it. Doing herself wrong felt so right.

It was... commitment. Commitment to being a slut. Which felt incredibly slutty. Which felt just right because... maybe she really was meant to be a slut....

That line of thinking, her jamming fingers, and then Esteban shooting his load on her face and Lynn's panties slung around her face combined to produce a singular orgasm. She felt weak all over and flopped forward which served her lust as she was able to lick at his shooting cock and swallow at least some of it down. It wasn't disgusting like it would have been before she came in this office. She wanted it. She wanted to do it. She wanted to do whatever Esteban wanted.

Laying on his skinny dark brown legs with her breasts hanging down she moved her mouth around licking up any sperm drops and streaks she could find with four fingers inside her pussy feeling her wet pussy sleeve flex and pulse and ripple in diminishing orgasm.

Esteban seemed impressed, "I knew you were a slut. Had no idea how much of one. You are as slutty as slutty can be. You're my new number one slut. For now. Until you get boring. You sluts always bore me eventually once you're totally broken in. I like a little challenge."

Why did that upset her? The idea of him getting bored and thus leaving her alone maybe should be a ray of hope. Instead the concept was almost devastating.

Well... she'd just have to try as hard as she could to please him.

Esteban pushed her aside and she crumpled to the floor. He cleaned himself with some tissues and got his clothing back in order. Then he plucked the yellow cat-head panties off her head. They had started off damp and now they had semen on them as well. He put them on a shelf behind some work manuals where she guessed the rest of his collection of waitress panties was stored.

"Get your bare ass up and pointed straight at the door. Make it higher than your head. You can touch yourself but no orgasm. I've got something for you. I'll be back in a while. Don't worry, I'll have Lisa cover your tables."

He left and Penny came more and more back to herself as her orgasm fully dissipated. As it did she felt more and more exposed. Feeling nude became feeling naked. Even worse than merely naked. Sweaty. Damp. Spots of semen here and there on her including in her hair which she knew had to be in disarray.

What if someone besides Esteban came back here and saw her like this?

She soon found out.

She heard the door open and a little yelp of surprise. Followed by speech.

"Holy shit! Who is that? Is that you, Lisa?"

Penny recognized Ariana's voice. She was too embarrassed to look over her shoulder. Besides, she didn't want Ariana to see the drying cum on her face. So she held position as she spoke.

"It's, uh, me. Penny."

"Holy shit! He got you, too! I mean, I can't throw stones in my glass house and all but I didn't think he'd ever nail you. I don't think he did either. Well, at least I won't have to wear your name tag while I blow him."

Ariana seemed to wait a few seconds for a reply but Penny said nothing. She had nothing to say. What could she say? She imagined she could feel Ariana's eyes on her ass and pussy. No doubt Ariana could see how wet she was. Nothing could be denied.

She heard Ariana leave and took a shaky breath of relief. She hoped Esteban would come back soon and tell her what to do next.

A minute later the door opened again and she heard a long gasp.

She couldn't help herself and she looked behind her. It was Patricia, the other new girl. Unlike Andrea, Esteban hadn't mentioned her so either he hadn't gotten around to nailing her or she'd turned him down.

Patricia's pretty face was twisted with frozen shock, "Penny? Is that you? What... what's going on?"

Penny just looked at her, unable to speak. Her bare ass, high in the air, was between them.

Patricia was a nervous talker and usually shared more than she should or intended, "I'm.. sorry! Ariana told me to come in here and ask Esteban where the stock of steak sauce is kept. Which is weird because all the tables have steak sauce as far as I could see.... Um, well, no Esteban so... I better get back to work."

Patricia closed the door.

Penny was angry at Ariana. That bitch! It was bad enough for Ariana to see her like this. But Ariana was involved in this kind of thing anyway. And she'd discovered Penny by accident. Setting up innocent Patricia to find her was just mean. To both her and Patricia. It did not bode well for Penny's reputation either. Patricia was such a talker. She'd tell everyone sooner or later. She wasn't mean. The girl just couldn't help herself.

Penny had a furtive nasty/hopeful thought very unlike herself. Maybe Esteban would nail Patricia before Patricia told people what she'd seen. Patricia wouldn't feel like casting stones if she'd done as much or even worse. Maybe Penny could even somehow put Esteban up to it...

Penny shook away the alien thought pattern. That was not who she was. No way. Maybe, just maybe, she was some kind of slut sexually. But that didn't mean she had to be a bad person morally or in how she treated others, especially an innocent like Patricia.

What was she thinking and what was she doing still in this totally compromised position?

The door opened again and this time it was Esteban.

It wasn't just him.

Also, Pablo!

"Mmm. Gracias, Esteban."

"No problemo, Pablo. Do as you wish."

Penny was in a state of shock as she heard Pablo unbuckle and drop his pants. She couldn't bring herself to look back at him. She was too embarrassed.

She heard him shuffle forward and heard the door close as Esteban left them alone.

Esteban had left to get her something. Apparently he'd meant Pablo's dick. She felt it bump up on her pussy.

Somehow her pussy felt as hot as her red embarrassed face. The two heats joined and fed off each other. Being so compromised was somehow both embarrassing and hot.

Being so aroused while Pablo made dick contact with her wetness was embarrassing. Being so humiliated made her hot. Everything was feeding off of each other.

She was, if anything, getting wetter.

It only took moments for Pablo to get fully hard. He felt much bigger than Esteban had felt in her mouth. He rubbed and rubbed and then suddenly inserted. He was big but he popped right in her hot wet receptive pussy.

Penny realized her pussy was not picky. None too discerning. It cared not at all that this cock was connected to an overweight heavy-eyebrowed dishwasher who could barely speak passable English.

Even if she was not a slut her pussy sure was. No way poor Pablo could tell the difference. It wasn't his fault. Esteban probably told him she was a slut and she was acting like a slut – pushing back against his penetration now – so how could he know? That really she wasn't?

She smelled his body odor even above the heavy smell of pussy and sperm gathered in the little room. His body odor got stronger as he really laid into her, grunting and sweating. It seemed like he was in a hurry.

Oh, yeah. His break was only ten minutes....

She rolled her hips and her pussy up and backwards. She realized she was doing it instinctively but also submissively because she wanted to give him a "good ride". Of course, the friction and the slutty behavior itself also increased her own pleasures.

The thought occurred he may shoot inside her. Probably would. Why wouldn't he?

She wasn't on protection. No boyfriend, no dates. Why take protection?

She wasn't sure where she was in her cycle. Too hard to bring today's date to mind. How did you say "protection" in Spanish?

This line of thinking seemed like a waste of time. She should be enjoying this fuck. If you're going to get fucked you should at least enjoy it.

It was also distracting her from something important. Something actually relevant.

Oh, yeah. Esteban before he left told her she could touch herself if she wanted. She sure as fuck wanted to now.

Penny used one hand to support herself – not easy with Pablo's weight rhythmically crashing into her with his belly overhang rippling along the top of her ass – and moved her right hand to finger and tease her clitoris.

The shock, the humiliation, the helplessness, the naughtiness, feeling like a slut, the big dirty cock in her pussy, and her own fingers combined to make a sum far greater than the parts.

She climaxed hard and screamed in pleasure. The thought of anyone hearing did not even enter her momentarily shrunken mind. If it had she would not have cared.

She slammed back so hard on Pablo that he almost staggered back and right out of her. He barely held his place by using his hands on her hips to hold inside her. Pablo reset and planted his cock as deep as he could, held it there, and shot his load right into her eagerly receptive womb.

Penny drove home with a clouded mind. She felt uplifted and oppressed, the two forces contesting for dominance.

Physically uplifted because her body was still humming from her orgasms.

Physically oppressed from an epic long day. A shift as a waitress was already pretty grueling and hard on the feet but she'd had her training session with Violet the Violent earlier in the day and all that back office sex with Esteban and Pablo as well.

She felt uplifted by those orgasms. She had not known they could feel that strong. Or that she could have that many in one day.

She felt oppressed by her own actions and what she'd allowed. Allowed? What she had enjoyed. Oppressed by future obligations as indicated by Esteban. What, she was supposed to go to work and just get fucked on a regular basis? By Esteban, Pablo, and supposedly Juan as well?

That didn't sound so bad as it really should....

None of the other waitresses would respect her now. Obviously. Then again, they were mostly doing the same stuff so she didn't respect them either. That's how she knew they wouldn't respect her.

She'd always sort of looked at Lynn as some form of inferior woman. She still thought that but now she was right there with her in that category.

Were Esteban, Violet, and Mr. Parker right to treat her the way they did? Right about her?

In the big picture was going from being a waitress with no sex life to a waitress/cheerleader/slut with multiple orgasms per day a downgrade or an upgrade?

There was more to it than that, of course. She had always been heterosexual until earlier that day with Violet. She had also always been monogamous. One lover at a time and almost always a boyfriend, not just casual sex.

Now, in such a short time span, she'd become a lesbian or, well, bisexual, and willing to engage in sex with multiple men in one day. Even with each other's knowledge! Even when she didn't find them attractive. Or even likable!

Always before, at the very least, likable was a requirement for fuckable. Of course, then it hadn't really been "fucking". It was just sex. Today... today was fucking.

She parked and got out of her hatchback. She couldn't even remember the drive home and felt lucky she made it safe. She felt drunk on sex.

She would not yet sober up once she got in her apartment.

She remembered she still needed Lynn to shave her pussy.

Was she still going to do that? Allow that?

Yes. Now more than ever.

She realized she was a mess down there. After Pablo came in her she'd started waiting tables, did that for hours, then, when told to, gave Pablo a blow job while Lisa gave Esteban a blow job. All of them crowded together in that little office. Her and Lisa's asses accidentally rubbing against each other again and again.

Once that "break" was over she'd been right back to work until closing time.

She thought she could feel Pablo's sperm squishing around in her vagina. She knew that feeling was just her imagination. She couldn't actually feel it. But she also knew his sperm really was in there. She desperately had to clean up before letting Lynn shave her down there.

She found out Lynn felt differently.

Lynn, in pink panties and a T-shirt, looked tired when Penny came in but perked up right away.

"Penny! I waited up for you."

"Oh. Uh. I need to get cleaned up."

"Don't worry about it."

"No. Really. I need to take a shower."

"Do that after."

"Lynn! Damn it, I've got Pablo's cum leaking out of me."

Lynn came over and started taking off Penny's clothing, "Like I said. Don't worry about it. I'm used to his cum."

Penny was too tired and felt too defeated by everything to put up any fight. Lynn rapidly got all of her clothing off. She pulled Penny by the hand into her bedroom and pushed her onto the bed on her back. She left and returned with a razor.

Penny was surprised when Lynn, one by one, produced thick nylon loops of rope from under each of the four corners of her bed. She cinched each one around one of Penny's wrists or ankles until she was bound and spreadeagled.

Penny felt dismay but no urge to protest. Once she allowed Lynn to take off her clothing she immediately entered that state of mind where she allowed whatever the other person wanted and did whatever the other person told her to do. Even little submissive Lynn.

At one point Lynn told her she was tying her down so she'd hold still while being shaved. For her own protection. It was a flimsy excuse at best and it wasn't even needed.   Penny would allow whatever.

Lynn got between her legs, laying on the bed. She held the razor but she didn't use it yet. She seemed to examine Penny's messy pussy in minute detail.

Lynn looked up at Penny with a mischievous grin, "I told you I'm used to Pablo's cum. I also like the taste of it."

With that Lynn applied her mouth to Penny's pussy.

It felt like she was trying to suck out all the cum!

After a couple minutes of sucking and licking Penny felt she might orgasm.

Her feeling was totally correct. She bashed her pussy into Lynn's cute face as her orgasm crashed. Then Lynn's face was as messy as Penny's pussy.

Afterward, Lynn slid up to Penny's face, gave her a sloppy kiss with tongue, then slid back down and tongued and licked Penny's pussy until Penny felt like she might orgasm yet again. It took a long time to get there but it felt like it was going to be another big one. But then Lynn stopped.

Lynn shaved her pussy and did a good thorough job while talking about how they had to try to avoid angering Mistress Violet even if they knew Mistress Violet would still find some excuse to punish them. It was their duty to try to obey her commands, not for personal gain or to avoid negative consequences, but just because Mistress Violet said so.

Once Penny was fully shaved and wiped clean Lynn went back down on her.

With a passion. It felt different but it felt just as good. Lynn licked yet another orgasm out of her.

Afterward Lynn looked up at her with a wet smile, "We should do this whenever we're not too tired from being used as sluts."

Penny decided not to say anything. She wanted to say this was a one time incident not to be repeated. But she wasn't confident that was true.

She didn't want to lie.

And she didn't actually see any reason why this should be only a one time event.

———————————————————————

Penny woke up late in the morning. Luckily, Lynn had removed her bindings while Penny slept – more like passed out from sexual exhaustion – because Lynn was already gone working another shift at Mack's. Probably already sucking a cock or taking a load in her pussy.

That line of thinking made Penny think less of Lynn. That line of thinking woke up her pussy. It began to heat up. Already! Again!

Penny realized these recent sexual events were not just her trying new things or trying to get kinks out of her system. They were becoming part of who she was. She was getting re-wired. Or... what was that phrase...?

Re-purposed. That was it. From hot but single picky and discerning waitress to submissive slut to just about anyone.

Fuck that.

Well, exactly.

It was in the shower when she finally stopped thinking about the day before – after masturbating herself – and suddenly thought about this day. No shift at Mack's but she was due at two-o-clock for more training with Violet. Violet the Violent. Mistress Violet. Mistress Violent.

That evil amazon bitch sure would be disappointed when she never showed up.

Right?

The thought did occur that she was going to have a hard time working at Mack's and stopping her slutty behavior. She couldn't live like that. Getting fucked several times a day by several different men, none of whom she liked or respected. None of whom had any potential to become a boyfriend or more.

If she left Mack's to be a full-time cheerleader she would still be getting used sexually. She knew that. She felt totally unable to stop these things at either location as long as she was going to them. It just wasn't in her.

But, at the least, she would then finally be out of the damn service industry!

She needed something with health insurance. That was the one redeeming feature of the cheerleading opportunity. She needed to find a job that had that but without requiring her to sexually debase herself.

She'd been thinking she could double her employment but maybe she would have to choose between the two. Temporarily. Until she could find something better without all that twisted sex.

After lunch, bored in the apartment, she really couldn't help but think about the terrible things Violet had done to her the day before.

Called her names.

Ordered her to have Lynn shave her pussy.

Made her strip.

Made her crawl naked.

Humiliated her.

Made her do lesbian things.

Denied her an orgasm... for a while.

Rode her like a pony.

Well....

Well... it hadn't really been *that* bad...

Thinking about the "terrible" incident made her hot and needy!

An hour later she walked into the stadium on time or maybe even a couple minutes early.

Don't want to be late for my abuse she thought with nervous bravado.

Penny couldn't believe she was doing it.

Violet wasn't in the room with the polished wood floor where she'd ridden Penny to orgasm the day before so Penny went to her office and knocked on the door.

There was a delayed response and then she heard permission to enter.

When Penny opened the door she saw Violet sitting behind a desk. It, too, was highly polished wood with nothing at all on it.

Nothing except a nude woman.

Well, she was partly on it. Her legs straddled one corner to Violet's right so the young woman more or less faced the door like Violet did. Her pussy was centered on the sharp desk corner and her torso lay diagonal across the smooth desk, her face turned sideways towards the door. Towards Penny.

The young woman humped the corner of the desk. Her pretty face twisted with helpless lust.

"Come on in, next slut." Violet motioned with her left hand for Penny to come forward while her right hand was on the bare ass of the young woman. A couple of Violet's fingers were buried in the ass crack of the nude woman and her arm was flexing.

Penny walked in. Violet had told her to, right? Couldn't say no to Violet, could she?

Penny could smell sex in the air. This other young woman really must be turned on. Seemed like it with how she was humping that desk corner. Penny wondered at that. It couldn't feel good and yet it sure looked like it did. That was certainly not the kind of thing Penny would ever do but, then again, no one would unless forced.

Obviously Violet had forced the poor girl. So this one was under Violet's command just like Penny. And like Lynn.

Penny wondered if she could really be a kindred spirit to a desk humper.

Then again, it was quite slutty and Penny had done quite a few slutty things herself recently.

Violet raised one eyebrow at her like she was waiting with amusement to see what Penny would say or do. Then she pulled her fingers out of the young woman's asshole and delivered a severe spank without looking away from Penny.

The young woman produced a weird gasp/wail and kept grinding on the desk corner, perhaps even grinding a bit harder.

Penny looked at the young woman. She was quite a spectacle. She had long straight brown hair and full breasts from what Penny could see of them as they bulged like water balloons under her weight and against the desk. A very pretty young lady. Sexy. All hot and bothered....

Violet interrupted Penny's reverie, "I'll be with you in a minute. Adria here, her session went a little long today. She's being trained just like you. Don't worry. I know you don't want to miss any of your special time with me. Your session will be extended as well. I won't cheat you out of what you need."

This Adria was being "trained just like" herself? That wasn't true at all. Sure, she'd been ridden like some sexual pony by Violet but at least she wasn't running around humping desks. Holy crap!

Violet delivered another severe blow to Adria's backside. Penny would have felt sorry for Adria but the woman kept reacting like she liked it. Sliding her breasts around, smearing sweat on the smooth polished wood of the desk. Keeping her pussy pressed on the presumably sharp corner and holding her place despite the spanks. Apparently getting off was more important to this Adria than stopping Violet from abusing her.

What a slut!

Almost impossibly Penny realized that one of the strongest feelings she was feeling right now – and there were a lot of strong ones – was jealousy.

She'd known Lynn had sex with Violet, of course, and she didn't even like Violet, of course, but this Adria was currently getting Violet's attention when right now it was supposed to be Penny's turn. For something. She realized she'd been looking forward to getting ridden or to licking Violet's pussy. Or whatever. Something.

Even a delay of just minutes suddenly seemed intolerable. Seeing this Adria so hot for it made Penny hot too.

Penny watched as Violet lived up to her nickname and delivered quite violent spanks every fifteen seconds of so. The poor girl's ass was red. The "poor girl" she was jealous of. Violet alternated between watching Adria's flexing ass and looking up at Penny's silently anguished face. She seemed to enjoy both equally and she smirk continuously.

Violet seemed to always know the right time to take action. And the right action to take. Penny couldn't really tell if Adria was getting closer to orgasm because she seemed sexually animated the entire time. But Violet could. Either that or she knew what would drive her over the edge.

Violet delivered one more powerful spank and then used that hand to abruptly insert two fingers back into Adria's asshole all the way in to the knuckle.

That was it. Adria groaned breathlessly like her lungs were collapsing and came on the corner of the desk. Adria ground her pussy on that corner like she didn't care if it did any damage to her.

Adria flopped about for half a minute before Violet became impatient, "Get going slut. More training tomorrow. Same time."

Adria slowly dismounted the desk, stumbled, and then recovered her balance. Then Adria stumbled about as she found articles of clothing and put them on. In the end they were embarrassingly askew. Her clothes and her face – and probably her smell – would at least strongly hint to anyone she ran into that she'd had a rather orgasmic time.

Adria hesitated and looked at the wet slick surface of the corner of the desk she'd been jamming against and sliding around on. She tentatively pointed a finger at the pussy juice.

Violet waved her off, "Don't worry about it. This other slut will clean it up."

Violet wasn't talking about her, was she?

Adria spoke in a submissive appreciative tone, "Thank you, Mistress Violet. See you tomorrow, Mistress Violet.

It was just so submissive, the words and the tone, that Penny was sure Violet must be quite pleased. Penny didn't think she could ever sound that submissive, that genuinely grateful for wrongs done upon her.

Which was good. Maybe.

It did sort of bother her, though, that this Adria was better than her - in that way - at pleasing Violet.

Because pleasing Violet served Penny's ends for the time being. Not for any other reason. Of course not.

Just before Adria left it turned out Violet had another task for Adria.

"Adria slut. You have a roommate?"

"Yeah, sure. I mean, yes, Mistress Violet."

"Tell me about her."

"She's going to college in mortuary science. I guess she's going to be a mortician."

"Don't care. How old is she and what does she look like?"

"She just turned twenty-one. She's very pretty, brownish-red hair. Sort of skinny but very pretty."

"Sounds like an excellent candidate for the cheer squad. Make sure she signs up. Send her to me. Really talk it up. Make up shit if you have to. Hell, tell her she'll get good health care. Tell her its a four star health plan with no copays. That works pretty good."

What!?! The health care was bullshit!?! Penny felt blazing anger, stiffening her back and her will. Health insurance was her reason for even being here at all! It was the reason she'd put up with so much. So much more than she ever should have.

"Mistress Violet... she has a boyfriend. They're serious."

"I'm serious, too. Boyfriend? What the fuck does that matter? Nothing. Not at all. You get her here – that's an order – and I take care of the rest."

"But... she's not just my roommate, she's my best friend."

"You don't want to sneak around behind your best friend do you? How long will she be your best friend once she finds out you're a submissive little pussy-licking bitch? She'll find out sooner or later. Better for you if she's a slut like you when she does. Besides, best friends are supposed to share things. Like having the same Mistress. Do it. See you tomorrow and I better see that roomie of yours by the end of the week."

Adria looked highly troubled but she gave the expected answer, "Yes, Mistress Violet."

Then she left.

Which left a furious Penny alone with Violet.

It wasn't just that there was no health care apparently and she'd fallen for the lie. That lie was told by Lynn. Which meant Lynn had done it at Violet's direction. Which meant the conversation she'd just seen play out between Violet and Adria also took place between Violet and Lynn.

Lynn had betrayed her! For sex! For abuse! At the command of this Mistress Violet creature!

Well, she couldn't beat up Violet, ex-wrestler Violet the Violent, but she could sure give her a piece of her mind.

"No health insurance? It's all a big fat lie?"

"Oooo, you look pissed off."

"You're a liar!"

"No, I'm not. Your roommate lied to you. If you've got a problem with that, take it up with her. Right now you need to get naked. Hop to it."

"Well, she may have lied to me but you obviously put her up to it."

"You're welcome."

"What?"

"You may never otherwise have become a cheerleader. Or the slut you really are. Would you really want to live a lie and be without someone better than you telling you what to do."

Violet put things in the most outrageous ways!

"As a matter of fact --"

"Do you really wish you missed out on those orgasms?"

Well... Penny had to admit Mistress Violet had a point there. She couldn't claim she hadn't liked the orgasms. No one could or should believe that. Penny would lose all credibility if she tried saying that to Violet. Mistress Violet would just laugh at her.

Violet waited a moment to see if Penny was going to speak, saw Penny frozen in thought, and then continued, " Tell me, do you really want to miss out on all the orgasms you know you'll have if you just be the slut you are and do as you're told by me or Parker?"

Penny thought that was a ridiculous question... and a good question.

Just like any attempt to claim she had not liked those orgasms would not fly so to any claim she would not like and want future orgasms. It would be hard to turn them down even if they didn't come with health insurance.

Violet's voice rushed into her decision vacuum, "Come over here. Right now."

That voice was so commanding that Penny was moving towards Violet and her slimy desk before she could even think whether or not to do as Violet ordered. She stopped just short of the edge of the desk. She only stopped when she obeyed Violet's order as much as possible.

The smell of pussy was much stronger this close.

Violet smiled in confident triumph.

Mistress Violet was pleased with her!

"Take off your clothes."

Violet almost began to do so but stopped herself. Taking off her clothes... just because Violet said so... that was pretty much committing herself right there... to all sorts of things. Including orgasms....

She looked nervously at Violet who was starting to look a bit stern.

She sure would hate to disappoint Mistress Violet....

Penny took clothes off starting at the top. Once she was naked from the waist up she dared a peek at Mistress Violet. Mistress Violet looked... interested.

The more clothes she took off and the more she felt Mistress Violet's eyes on her, appraising and appreciating, the hotter Penny became. The heat of anger transformed into a different kind of heat.

As Penny got her last sock off she caught a look at her pussy. It looked swollen and wet and surprisingly bare thanks to the intimate shave Lynn gave her the night before. She thought Mistress Violet would be gratified her order was followed. Penny was actually excited to see her reaction.

Penny straightened up, stood tall, and thrust out her big breasts. She adopted what she supposed would be a posture that would please Mistress Violet.

Penny saw that Mistress Violet did indeed look at her shaved pussy and gave a little nod of recognition that her order was followed. It was such a quick look and such a little nod but it made Penny's pussy flood with juices. Mistress Violet continued to survey her and seemed to be in no rush.

Penny always disliked being appreciated for her physical charms alone. It was so objectifying. She generally covered and minimized her breasts for instance. At the beach, the rare times she made it there, she usually wore a tank top over her swim suit top. For that reason alone.

Suddenly, here and now, she was highly aroused being examined like this. Nothing hidden. Her body being visually enjoyed. By a nasty mean amazon but, still, enjoyed.

For the moment at least she was a sexual object and the sexual object was happy to be what it was.

Penny had almost been the opposite of an exhibitionist but now, for the first time, she could see how someone could be aroused by it. Because she was right then. The fact her bare pussy was wet and Mistress Violet could see she was wet – her pussy could no longer keep a secret – was also a turn on.

There was more to her arousal. She knew Mistress Violet would soon give her directions – orders – on nasty things to do. Things she had to do. Things she would do. Things she never would have done if she hadn't found someone willing to treat her like a sex toy.

It was amazing to her that she'd been so angry at Mistress Violet just a minute ago. Full of righteous indignation at being fooled. All that anger was gone now, replaced by much more welcome lust.

It was her fault anyway. She blamed herself. Who would ever believe cheerleaders for some start up sports league got full health insurance?

If she really wanted health insurance she just needed to go to any other developed nation in the world. Becoming a cheerleader in America was a preposterous way to get health insurance. She was the stupid one who believed the lie so she was the one to blame.

Penny looked down at her breasts. She guessed they were going to stay big for the foreseeable future. Maybe even forever. Maybe she just needed to accept them. Mistress Violet liked them. Mr. Parker liked them. Why couldn't she like them, too?

Mistress Violet stood up and Penny's breath caught in anticipation.

Anything.

Whatever she wanted.

Maybe Mistress Violet would even forgive her for getting angry at her.

The amazon leaned across the desk, reached out, and grabbed a handful of Penny's dark hair. Penny had a lot of hair on her head so she had a lot of handholds for Violet to choose from. Violet pulled her in and down and towards her.

In seconds nude Penny was half-laying across the polished desk with her toes barely touching the floor and her hard nipples on the hard wood surface pushed back into her big soft breasts.

Penny's instinct to struggle, to resist, fought her instinct to obey and put up with whatever the dominant woman did. Her instinct to resist lost that momentary battle.

"Nice job shaving that hot pussy of yours. I guess that slut Lynn gets the credit though. Here is what you're going to do. Slide that sexy ass of yours over and get that hot slut pussy of yours on the corner of desk across from me and to my right. Since you're such a stupid slut I guess I should also explain that my right is your left. Get that pussy on that corner and then commence to pussy polishing it."

Penny slid to obey. She knew there was no getting out of this with Mistress Violet having a handful of her hair. And an even bigger handhold of her soul.

Penny wasn't even sure she wanted to get out of it. She was suddenly quite curious what that hard wood corner would feel like on her pussy. Her pussy needed something but it wouldn't be able to get much penetration there.

She slid her pussy into place. The corner spread her pussy lips most pleasingly. She marveled at how nasty this was. How humiliating. Hadn't she just thought less of Adria for being a "desk humper"? Now, here she was, a desk humper also.

That wasn't quite true...

Without direction from Mistress Violet she went ahead and rolled her pussy against the sharp corner.

There. Now she was a desk humper. Just like Adria. A slut just like Adria.

It could be even worse. This corner was fresh and dry. Or it was before her own pussy began soaking it. At least she wasn't humping the same corner Adria had. Gross. Germs. Plus, she was on the far side so Mistress Violet couldn't spank her. Yet another plus.

She jammed her pussy on the sharp corner as Mistress Violet watched her with amusement. It was a strange sensation. The corner could barely penetrate yet it spread her pussy lips incredibly wide.

She felt like pussy juice was running out of her. There were even wet sounds coming from her pussy grinding that corner. Her pussy juice must be running down the two sides of the desk that met there.

Her breasts slid back and forth like they were trying to wash the desk. It got moist under them as well from her perspiration. It felt so good on her nipples. That hard slick surface. That evaluating gaze of Mistress Violet.

"Yes. Your training is going so well." Violet put the emphasis on "so" and really oozed out verbal satisfaction. It increased Penny's humiliation. It increased Penny's arousal. Penny was coming to realize the two were one and the same.

It didn't seem like Mistress Violet expected any answer so Penny kept breathing hard while doing rapid mini-thrusts of her pussy onto the desk corner. The bent forward position and the way the edges of the desk kept her pussy lips spread so wide meant her clitoris slid around on the polished wood desk top. The sensations were off the charts and her gasps got louder and faster.

"Make yourself useful, slut. Clean that other desk corner."

Penny looked around for a cloth or tissues but the desk top was bare.

"With your slut mouth, stupid slut."

Oh. Penny did feel sort of stupid for not realizing that. Of course. Use her mouth. So simple. So... direct.

Also so wrong!

Licking up the other cheerleader's pussy juice was sort of gross. But. on the scale of things. not nearly as bad as disobeying a direct order by Mistress Violet. That would be just plain wrong whereas licking up a near stranger's pussy juice... that was more like a gray area.

Wasn't it said, maybe in the Bible, that sometimes you had to choose the lesser of two evils? Surely disobeying Mistress Violet was a greater evil than licking up some stranger's pussy juice from a desk top....

Penny twisted her body and brought her face down and the odor of evaporating pussy juice was quite a turn on. Either that or the sliding of her clitoris on the desk top was doing something to her. Probably both were.

Penny found herself wanting to know how Adria's pussy juice tasted. She hoped it hadn't mixed with wood polish and lost its own taste.

Awkwardly, with her torso contorted to her left, she began licking the desk surface. Everywhere it was at all wet or damp.

The process was made even more difficult by Mistress Violet using a handful of her hair as a handle and directing her face back and forth. It was more difficult because Mistress Violet often cruelly pressed down and squashed her face into the slickness she was trying to swipe up with her mouth. Penny thought that was mean but Mistress Violet was the boss. Whatever she wanted Penny also wanted. If Mistress Violet wanted her face squashed onto drying pussy juice on her desk top then that's what Penny wanted too.

Mistress Violet used her hair handle to move her face over to what was nearly a pool of pussy juice near that corner of the desk, "Suck that up, slut. Vacuum it up with your pretty little slut mouth."

Penny applied suction and slurped it up. The taste wasn't strong but it was good. The humiliating naughtiness was better.

Mistress Violet had her licking and sucking long after there was any real amount of Adria's pussy juice left.

Penny kept humping the desk edge. She was close but knew Mistress Violet probably wanted her to wait to orgasm until told to. So she kept herself on edge both literally and figuratively and paced herself.   She didn't mind. She knew now that the longer she kept herself just short of orgasm the more powerful it would be.

Mistress Violet stood up and released her hair hold. Then she moved around behind Penny. Penny could not see her and wondered anxiously what she would do.

A few spanks landed quickly and harshly. Penny maintained her position though the spanks drove her onto the desk corner as did her instinct to move away from them. They made her grind harshly on it which hurt more than the spanks.

Mistress Violet continued to spank and Penny quickly realized the pain, the outrage of it, the humiliation, and the crushing of her pussy against the desk edge were all greatly increasing her arousal. She couldn't control it and she couldn't stop it.

Penny wailed and climaxed on the desk edge. Her torso flopped on the desk top, her big breasts slid around, her ass tilted up to receive more spanks with the skin across her ass stretched tight to increase the pain.

An unknown but short time period later Penny came back to herself. She had not really passed out but she hadn't been aware of her surroundings either.

Mistress Violet was back in her chair behind the desk looking at her, "Did you enjoy your orgasm, slut?"

It was a stupid question thought Penny. Who didn't enjoy orgasms?

"Yes, Mistress Violet."

"You should have waited until I gave you permission."

Penny agreed even though Mistress Violet had not actually ordered her to hold it. She wanted to defend herself and tell Mistress Violet how she just could not help herself. But, of course, Mistress Violet probably already knew that and, of course, Mistress Violet was not one to accept any excuses no matter how legitimate.

"Yes, Mistress Violet. I'm sorry, Mistress Violet."

"Well, try, try, try again I say." Mistress Violet stood up and Penny saw that she was now wearing a strap-on dildo.

Violet moved behind Penny, "Get back to desk fucking, slut."

Tentatively at first Penny began humping the desk corner again. The corner and desk surface under Penny were slick with her pussy juice and perspiration. Her pussy seemed eager to get right back to it.

Penny felt Mistress Violet's hands on her sore and sensitive ass cheeks, "Have you ever been DPed? That stands for "double penetration". That's what we'll do now. Me and Mr. Desk. Of course, since Mr. Desk has your pussy I'll just have to take your ass."

Her ass!?! Penny tried anal sex once long ago with a boyfriend. She'd given in to his pleas and, really, more to the beers she'd drank. She had not liked it at all.

Was she going to tell Mistress Violet her ass was off limits?

Hell no. Nothing was off limits with Mistress Violet. Penny could not deny her anything. As had already been proven.

She was so hot and such a slut she almost thought she'd end up liking it anyway. Almost.

She felt Violet spread her ass cheeks and felt the knobby end of the dildo tapping at her asshole. She heard a spitting sound and then felt wetness on her asshole. Violet used the head of the cock-shaped dildo to rub the spit around.

"Ask me politely to ass fuck you."

Penny did not hesitate to obey, "Will you please fuck my ass, Mistress Violet?"

"Sure, slut."

Violet began working the dildo into Penny's ass and it took quite a bit of effort. It didn't help that Penny humped a little on the desk corner despite trying to hold still for the dildo. Her body slid around on the desk surface and Violet had a hard time maintaining her grip on Penny's ass cheeks.

It took effort and work, different species of grunting from both, and a great deal of discomfort for Penny but, in the end – Penny's rear end – they teamed up, each playing their role, to get the large dildo somehow all the way up Penny's ass.

"All the way in, desk fucker!" Violet slapped Penny's ass three times quickly.

Penny could barely breath from the strength of her lust. All the way in? That dildo was all the way in? She felt full and stretched and it was uncomfortable and it even hurt. She loved it. She felt a giddy triumph. Of course, Mistress Violet really deserved all the credit.

"Fuck your ass back on my plastic dick and fuck your pussy on Mr. Desk. Try to make us cum."

That was a bizarre and unrealistic expectation. Even so, Penny did her best to make the impossible happen. She bucked back and forth and fervently hoped Mistress Violet's plastic dick and Mr. Desk would orgasm. She tried and tried with several minutes of high effort.

"Cross the finish line, desk fucker." Mistress Violet gathered some of Penny's long hair by winding it round and round her fist while using her other hand to push down on the small of Penny's back. Then she pulled back on Penny's hair which made her head go back and popped her damp breasts out from under her as her torso reared up.

Then Violet really went to town rapidly slamming the plastic cock in and out of Penny's loosened ass. The hand pushing down on the small of Penny's back increased the contact between Penny's sliding clitoris and the slick desk which exponentially increased Penny's pleasures.

That was enough. That was plenty.

Penny screamed as she had another, even greater, orgasm. The biggest and longest she'd ever had.

She wasn't even able to experience all of it or fully appreciate it. Not once she passed out.

Penny came to on the carpet of the office.

Right away Mistress Violet had her thank her for the orgasm. Her gratitude was real and her thanks was sincere. Just looking at Mistress Violet made her feel warm and fuzzy.

Mistress Violet had her clean off the plastic cock. With her mouth, of course. Penny did not mind. It seemed like the natural way of things.

The plastic of the dildo was still quite warm in her mouth so Penny figured she had not been passed out long at all.

Then Mistress Violet had her go into a little bathroom adjoining the office and had her brush and floss her teeth and then gargle with a gentle mouthwash. Penny found this strange but it was not her place to ask questions.

When she came out she saw Mistress Violet, sitting in her chair, no longer wore the strap-on and was naked from the waist down.

Mistress Violet spread her legs and pointed at the carpet between them. The office carpet or her pubic hair, it could have been either one, or both, but she definitely pointed at carpet.

Oh, so that was why Mistress Violet wanted her mouth nice and clean....

Penny went where directed and did the obvious. She orally pleasured Mistress Violet. She put in her best effort. She found she wanted to do a good job. A great job. She wanted to please Mistress Violet. It was her mission. It was more important than anything.

She felt like Mistress Violet should be rewarded for making her fuck a desk. And for making her suck up pussy juice from the desk. And for spanking her. And for ass fucking her. And for taming her. And for letting her lick her pussy.

For making her into a submissive slut or for recognizing it in her and tapping into it. Whichever.

After a few minutes Mistress Violet climaxed wetly but quietly. She told Penny to bring her off a second time.

Penny worked hard at that. Somewhere in that process the door opened.

It was Mr. Parker!

"Violet, sorry for the interruption. I see you're in a training session."

"No problem, Parker. What can I, or, more likely, one of the cheerleader sluts, do for you?"

"The parking lot was a bit muddy today and I may also have stepped in something of an organic nature. Not sure what. So my shoes need a good thorough cleaning. Do you suppose...?"

"Of course, Parker. No problem. I'll have this one finish up and she'll be right over to your office."

So it went. After Mr. Parker left it took Penny about five more minutes of furious passionate licking before Mistress Violet came again.

Then Penny got dressed and went to Mr. Parker's office and took care of cleaning his shoes while he wore them and while he talked on the phone.

It was weird, to say the least. It felt so... normal. Even though it wasn't and it was only her second time doing that kind of humiliating task. But she had done dozens of embarrassing or humiliating or nasty things in recent days so it was just one more. Besides, Mistress Violet expected her to do it and Mr. Parker wanted her to do it so... who would hold it against her?

The shoes were gritty and there was some dried mud smears on the sides but nothing "organic"... as far as she could tell or taste.

Mr. Parker didn't make it easy on her either with how he wiggled and waved the shoes as he was distracted with phone conversation. He talked to someone about additions to stock and the condition of the stock and when some stock would be available for market. Seemed like a strange thing to talk about since he was a manager of a sports team. Apparently he also dealt in cattle.

The toe of his shoe bumped her chin as something in his phone conversation caught his attention, "What kind of tricks?"

Penny sucked the end of one shoelace clean, sort of rolling it in a mouthful of saliva like a sideways washing machine as she wondered what kind of tricks cattle could ever do. She could not hear what the person on the other end was saying to

Parker.

"Yes, of course, that. You'd be surprised. They will be able to do more than you even could expect or hope. But, obviously, anything very unusual you'd have to arrange with us first. That kind of preparatory effort would require a prepayment in case you were not the end buyer. Nothing for free you know. Not truly."

Bizarre. Penny couldn't think why anyone would want "stock" to do any tricks. Cattle were for meat and cows were for milk. No tricks involved. Who would pay to have them taught specific tricks for them to do before they were milked or slaughtered?

Penny tried not to even figure it out. Not her business anyway. Plus, it was hard to think now that she was tonguing the heel of his leather shoe because it was vertical on her face so while she sucked and licked the rest of the dirty sole was bouncing on her nose and forehead. It was not very conducive for processing thoughts.

After listening a while Mr. Parker spoke again, "I'm sure a private viewing and some personal handling can be arranged. View the stock all together and just let me know which ones you want to get to know first hand."

Apparently Mr. Parker was talking to some kind of weirdo. Who would want to "get to know" a dairy cow or cattle? Well, none of Mr. Parker's business was any of her business. She was just a lowly shoe slut. She really had no room to criticize anyone at all.

Soon after, Mr. Parker ended the call and leaned back in his chair with his legs stretched out. Since his shoes were then on the office carpet balanced on their heels Penny had to lean way down sometimes with her cheek on the carpet to continue her oral cleaning of the shoes.

This also meant her ass was relatively high. She felt Mr. Parker avail himself of that situation as he leaned up and felt her ass lightly.

She hadn't given him permission for that kind of personal touch but who was she kidding anyway. It was obvious to both of them he could do anything he wanted and she would just allow it. It was like the word no was no longer part of her vocabulary. At least once she got into any sort of sexual situation.

She was licking and sucking and kissing on his shoes! What, then, wouldn't she do?

This shoe-licking was a sexual act to her. She had to acknowledge it. It made her indescribably hot. It was just so submissive and so humiliating. That made it as hot as could be.

His touching her ass made her feel good. It was a compliment really. An important man like Mr. Parker wanting to touch her ass. He wouldn't touch it if he didn't like it. How it looked. Hopefully he liked how it felt as well.

Maybe... he'd want to do something with her after she finished cleaning his shoes? If she did a good job on them?

His hand moved to the clothing covered furrow of her pussy and rubbed up and down.

"Did you spill some more water down here? From your water bottle?"

Penny hadn't thought she could get more embarrassed than she already was – licking shoes clean – but she felt her face flush red and not all of it was from the blood rushing to her inverted head as she struggled to get her tongue to the muddy grit on the angle between the heel and arch.

Mr. Parker obviously remembered their previous encounter when she had tried to blame her wet pussy on a water bottle spill. He also obviously knew she was once again hot and bothered and very wet from basically going down on his shoes.

It was some consolation that at least he remembered her. That was something.

She thought he may want a response, "No, sir. Not a spill from a water bottle."

"What's your name again?"

He didn't remember her very well after all. She was licking all the mud and slime from his shoes and he didn't even know her first name!

"Penny, sir."

"So, it's true what they say. Finding a Penny head's down is even better luck than one that is heads up."

Very funny. She'd never heard that one before, had she?

This time it had a different effect though. Instead of angering her it was just pure patronizing humiliation. Which... was a good thing. The heat in her pussy blazed. His stroking fingers stoked the blaze even higher. She found herself arching her pussy up to increase contact and to let Mr. Parker know she appreciated his attentions.

"You know, I'm giving you all this nasty pleasure, even letting you lick my shoes. I think you should be more grateful." His stroking hand slowed its pace to something like slow motion. Too slow to get there!

His hint was obvious. She might be a dumb slut but she wasn't a stupid slut.

"Thank you, sir. For letting me clean your shoes. And for... touching me." Her voice was muffled by shoe but he heard her and went back to stroking, more firmly now.

She was close! How had it happened so fast?

"There's the proper gratitude. It's very important for a creature like you to show gratitude to its betters. Your betters being basically everyone."

It was so awfully humiliating!

It was working on her mind.

She was so close. She needed it so bad.

"I will reward you."

A reward! Yes! He was going to let her orgasm!

He pulled his hand away and used his foot to push her head away from its shoe servicing.

"Stand up for a moment. Take your clothes off. The ones at waist level and below."

Penny was disappointed at the delay. No immediate satisfaction for her. But taking off her clothes sounded promising. Would he perhaps bend her over his desk and fuck her? Could she be that lucky?

No.

Finally, not quickly enough for her preference, she wore only her sports bra and top and stood before him awaiting direction. He briefly scanned her shaved-clean pubic area. Which was quite wet and swollen with arousal.

Then he scanned each of his shoes in turn, carefully lifting each foot and turning the shoe this way and that.

"You did an adequate job, Penny the shoe slut. They are nice and shiny. Now that is what I call a spit shine! Still. They could use a good buffing. They could really do with a good solid pussy buffing. Some vaginal oils to infuse the leather. It will put such a warm shine to the leather. Go ahead. I'll let you do it. This is your reward for adequate work in service to one of your betters."

Seriously?

But she knew he was.

And... somehow... it didn't sound that crazy.

Her pussy wanted, needed, contact and here Mr. Parker was kindly offering a direct avenue to facilitate that.

She nearly thanked him. He would have liked that but she couldn't stand any delay.

Now was her chance to buff his shoes with her bare hot wet needy pussy!

She had never wanted anything like that ever before, hadn't heard of such a thing, and hadn't known she even could want it, but she was desperate for it now.

Penny fell to her knees and shuffled forward until she straddled his right shoe. She was intent on doing something very wrong on that right shoe.

Her legs hugged either side of his foot and she lowered her pussy down to it and began working it on the leather. On the shoe laces. Even on his plaid dress socks peaking above the tongue of the shoe.

She wasn't sure what all needed to be buffed on a shoe so she tried to buff all surfaces. She had plenty of pussy juice. No shortage issue there.

She came the first time as she began to pussy buff his left shoe after finishing the right one.

Once she recovered she went back to buffing.

She was almost done and quite aroused again when he spoke again, "Shoe slut. Get the toe of my shoe up your dirty pussy and fuck it. Fuck that shoe!"

Penny hopped to it. It struck her as a brilliant idea by Mr. Parker.

Fuck her pussy on the tip of his shoe! Of course!

It was all too easy to move her pussy down to the angled toe tip, aim it hurriedly, and then slide down onto it. It pushed her pussy lips to either side as her own weight worked to impale her pussy on the blunt leather tip.

It stretched her wider than the desk corner had and she was swollen and sore from that desk corner. The pain was a strong surprise but not unwelcome as it brought tremendous simultaneous pleasure.

The combined sensations produced a long troubled groan from her.   It made her pause, not with hesitation or self-awareness, but with surprised adaptation to all the sensations. She felt pussy stretched again but this time the toe tip was getting more depth and the leather was more rounded and softer than the hard desk.

"Ride that shoe, shoe slut. Ride it like it's your pony."

Penny began working her pussy up and down, trying to get the shoe as deep as possible. It already was so all that accomplished was more hurt which, for some reason, was actually quite rewarding.

She looked down and saw her poor pussy lips stretched and red and struggling to envelop the shoe, a struggle it could never win, only lose joyfully. Pussy juice ran down the shoe and into the carpet.

Penny slammed her pussy up and down. She was lost in the shoe fucking process.

Until she looked up and saw too-old too-nerdy Mr. Parker watching her with great amusement.

She felt a moment of total self-awareness. Fucking a shoe. She was fucking a shoe. While this near stranger wore the shoe! She was doing it just because he told her to!

She felt intense shame. What would people she knew think of her if they saw her now?

It wasn't quite the full truth that she did it because Mr. Parker told her to. She also wanted to do it. She needed to do it. She was happy to do it. She was grateful he allowed her to do it.

Those feelings were, in a way, more shameful than the actual act. Loving what she should hate was maybe worse than doing what should not be done.

Seeing him watching her with a tolerant patient amused look on his face intensified her shame. Which was why she kept looking at him. The greater the shame the greater the pleasure.

Wrong or not, it just was how it was.

She wasn't sure why she hadn't noticed before but she noticed now. Mr. Parker had that smart phone of his out again but he wasn't talking on it. She realized when the back of it faced her like it did now he could be making a video of what she was doing.

Was he?

A better question might be, why wouldn't he?

A man who would make you lick his shoes clean or make you (let you) fuck his shoes wouldn't have any moral qualms about making a video of it, would he?

She had a momentary flashback to her first time cleaning his shoes with her mouth. How he'd held his smart phone then with the back of it always facing her.

He wasn't keeping her from seeing what was on the face of it! He was recording what she did! Her engaged in kissing, licking, tonguing, and sucking his shoes!

She should be mad. She should be so mad.

Forgiveness bubbled up in her in the form of the bubbling heat in her pussy.

Why wouldn't he? Why shouldn't he? How could she blame him?

It really wasn't her place to blame him for anything was it? A lowly shoe slut was no one to judge anyone, was she?

Getting upset might ruin this orgasm she needed.

She had never told him not to video her. Sure, he hadn't asked, but... she never told him not to.

She knew she was quite a sight.

People he told about her shoe licking and shoe fucking probably wouldn't believe him if he didn't have evidence. So... he just needed to do it.

Maybe it was sort of a compliment. Preserving her sexy shoe fucking for posterity.

She rode the shoe harder. The idea of being in a sex video debasing herself was a huge turn on! She hadn't thought she could get more aroused but she was. She knew she definitely would have come by now if she wasn't so wore out. Wore out but still energized with some alien energy outside herself.

"Don't go all monogamous on me. Or on my shoes. I think my right shoe is jealous of my left you're riding. You pussy buffed the right one but you've pussy buffed and fucked the left. Share the pussy. Menage a trois of the shoes. You're a shoe-sexual."

Penny pulled her pussy off his left shoe and plopped down onto his right. She felt lustful relief once she had that shoe tip trying to fill her. It was like leaving a pool of warm water for a moment and then getting back into it.

She loved the hateful way he spoke down to her. Down to her literally and figuratively.

She looked up and saw the smart phone still pointed at her.

An idea occurred and, before she could stop herself, she played up to the phone, looking straight into its tiny viewfinder, "I'm a shoe fucker. A nasty shoe fucker. Thank you, sir, for letting me fuck your shoes!"

She had just purposely humiliated herself even more....

Penny climaxed, viciously jamming her pussy down onto Mr. Parker's right shoe tip.

She released a gurgling wail.

She released a flood of pussy juice.

She went weak all over and flopped backwards onto the carpet and off his shoe.

She lay there in a dark afterglow. She heard some beeps. His phone.

She heard some more beeps a few moments later and then Mr. Parker was speaking, but not to her. He was leaving a voice mail.

"I just sent you a video. Let me know how you like that trick and if you're interested in that sort of thing."

Had he sent the video of her shoe fucking to someone? Already?

When he'd talked about "stock" earlier... was she "stock"?

Then he had her get dressed and told her to leave.

She opened the door to leave but looked at him. To see if he wanted anything else from her. Or to get final permission to leave.

"If that's all, sir." Inwardly she rolled her eyes at herself. She sounded like a butler! Was she that subservient? Yes. She was.

"Yes, Penny. When you're done with your training with Violet tomorrow come back by this office and I'll make use of your shoe-cleaning service again. In fact, do that every time you train."

"Yes, sir."

So, he was just going to pretend like all this was some kind of normal!

"If you do a good job again I'll give you a tip. Actually, I'll give you your tip beforehand tomorrow but it will be for today. It will have to be the next day each time and before each time."

Penny was mystified and he saw that on her face.

"The tip being the tip of my cock, of course. It has to be before you clean my dirty shoes with your slut mouth. For obvious reasons of hygiene. But you'll get to suck my cock and then you can lick clean my shoes. A double reward for a shoe slut like you."

But... but... but she was only a shoe slut because he made her do those things!

She left his office flooded with the thrill of total wrongness.

Every day she trained from now on he expected her to lick clean his shoes after she sucked his cock...?

If he wanted it she was just sure she was going to do it. Hard to say no to those wrong but powerful orgasms.

Arriving back at her apartment, Penny began to feel differently. She was coming back to her own little world. Her stuff. Her privacy. Her domain. Not fancy but... still. It was independent living.

She knew what she should do. Never ever go back to that stadium again. Try to forget it all.

Move out and away from living with Lynn.

Just say no to Esteban and friends while she found a new job. Hell, everywhere needed a waitress willing to put up with shit. Which she was willing to do, just not nearly so much as she had been.

Do all that and, presto, the old Penny returns victorious. Or, at least, not in an ongoing state of shame.

She was relieved Lynn was at work and would be until late. She wasn't sure if she didn't want to see her because she was so angry at her for totally selling her out, or because Lynn might expect a repeat of the night before (which Penny was not at all sure she could turn down), or because she felt so humiliated.

It might be hard to go from bound and pussy licked to casually chatting roommate. Or scolding roommate.

She ate, watched a few shows, and just felt bored more than anything. After all the sex, bizarre sex, good sex... great sex... everything paled by comparison.

It couldn't be helped. Her mind replayed it all. All of it, not just favorite parts.

It was all favorite parts actually.

Round and round her actions and reactions went in her mind. She couldn't keep track of the shows she was watching.

She felt stupider from all her mind-blowing orgasms.

One thing was clear. Incredibly, she was horny all over again.

She went to her bedroom and lay back on propped up pillows. She rubbed herself through her panties, then took them off and went back to it.

She fingered and rubbed for a long time.

She was more aroused than normal when she masturbated. She used her usual sliding finger thrusts and clitty flicking which generally worked quite well.

She knew she could have an orgasm this way. Would have an orgasm this way.

But it just felt so vanilla.

There was no twist to it. Nothing nasty.

She was still replaying scenes from her time with Violet the Violent and Mr. Parker and they were nasty and twisted. The problem now was that her own actions were not.

She could have an orgasm as is. But there was a way to have a bigger orgasm....

As soon as the thought occurred to her she knew she was going to do it. Just was.

Bottomless, she dashed out of her bedroom to the front door. She and Lynn weren't too cleanly but they did leave their shoes at the door when they came home. There was a pretty big partially organized pile of footwear there.

She had thrown out her pair of fancy boots after she left a bite mark in one of them while masturbating. Damn. She should have kept them. Not for wearing though. Just under her bed.

Her tennis shoes? Sandals? No and no. None of her others seemed right for the planned wrong either.

Then she noticed Lynn's boots that were similar boots to the ones of hers that she'd thrown out except these were brown, not black. It was Lynn's fault, to at least some extent, that Penny was now some kind of "shoe slut". So... law of unintended consequences applied.

Sorry, Lynn! You little bitch!

Penny grabbed one boot, turned back to her room, had an inspiration, turned back and grabbed the other one as well and brought both back to her bedroom.

She eagerly flopped back in place propped up on the pillows. She felt a nausea in her tummy that was almost sexual. Like she wasn't sure if she was going to puke or orgasm.

She got the tip of one of Lynn's leather boots up against her pussy. She thought it was the left boot. She marveled at how slutty she was as she pressed it in. Hard.

It couldn't get very far but it did feel great. Also, as Lynn had slimmer feet, she knew it was further in than she would have managed with her own footwear. She worked it in and out in very short thrusts.

She accidentally found she could sort of lever it, bopping it up and down, and the rounded toe tip would tap at her G-spot.

Right away she was so very close.

But she thought she knew how to make the orgasm even bigger than what it would be as is.

The desire for orgasm, the best of orgasms, ruled her absolutely.

Thoughts of being a shoe slue did not give her any pause at all. It turned her on! She was a filthy shoe slut!

Penny brought the other boot up to her nose and sniffed the outside. A little stinky. Her pussy gripped greedily at the first ones toe tip.

She couldn't afford to put the tip in her mouth. She couldn't afford it financially. She might end up leaving bite marks and then she'd have to throw them out. She couldn't afford to buy Lynn a new pair.

She turned the boot and stuck the top on her nose and mouth like a gas mask. She inhaled.

Very stinky! She pressed the other boot with all her strength against her pussy.

In moments Penny had a huge orgasm.

A butt-bouncing head-thrashing orgasm.

Later, just before she fell sleep, she remembered thinking, "Yeah, I'm going back to the stadium tomorrow."

Penny did go back the following day and every day after that seven days a week. For quite a while she did.

Mr. Parker did give her a tip that day and very often thereafter. As promised, the tip of his cock. The rest of it as well. Then she would lick his shoes clean with almost religious concentration and dedication. Then, of course, buff them with her pussy. Shined them with her orgasmic juices as it always made her orgasm.

He was often on the phone but talked a lot more about promising stock than he did the team. She always wondered exactly what or who the stock were. She did have her suspicions.

Sometimes her duties were shared. She couldn't selfishly claim all the shoe slut duties as her own, could she? Lynn and her held hands to great orgasms sometimes while they each pussy buffed a shoe. Other times it was other cheerleaders. She saw Liana sometimes, the young woman who had tried out with her. She looked quite sexy riding a shoe. Her training was obviously coming along just as well as Penny's.

Liana also took a whipping surprisingly well. She just hung in the ropes patiently while the whip landed, like a sexual martyr. It was Violet the Violent who liked to whip them.

She whipped Penny as well. Penny had mixed feelings about that. It hurt like hell but always led to even more powerful orgasms so... why not be whipped? The marks it left did concern her though. She needed to be ready to cheer for the team and the fans.

There were eight cheerleaders on the cheer squad at first but eventually six more girls joined including both Lisa and wide-eyed Patricia from Mack's.

Mack's, and Esteban, would need to do some hiring. She and Lynn had also quit. Trying to become the best cheerleaders they could be – and the best shoe sluts and best in general sluts – took a lot of time and dedication.

For a couple weeks Penny had been used and really enjoyed being used by the male staff at Mack's. It was nasty and wrong so that made it good. But she only had so much time. Being a cheerleader was the key to unlocking her future. She just knew it even though her vision of the future was cloudy at best.

Esteban and Pablo and Juan would find new girls to hire and exploit. She refused to feel sorry for them.

To save time Mistress Violet often had training sessions for the whole cheer squad. Except for Violet, they were all nude during these sessions. She often lined them up asses in the air and went from one to the next one whipping them and fingering them. When they got close to orgasm she left them hanging.

She only gave a few orgasms each day. To those who were the most obedient, the hottest in their reactions, or by some other secret calculus of her own. All the girls competed for those precious orgasms. Sure, they could give themselves or each other orgasms later but it meant more to get one from Mistress Violet.

Then one or two of them would go to service Mr. Parker's shoes. And his cock. All the cheerleaders now called him Master Parker though for some maybe Parker was his first name and others Parker was his last name.

Penny found herself obsessing about Master Parker's cock. Which was odd because it was very average in every way. Every way except availability. Penny knew 99.9% of all men – all heterosexual men – if single would be happy to stick their cock in her pussy. Master Parker was the one tenth of 1%.

She hinted at it politely, oh so politely, when she could, when her mouth wasn't stuffed with shoe or spouting self-humiliating profanity, how much she'd love to be fucked by him, how much she wanted his cum shot up her pussy.

She even brought it up with Lynn. Lynn told her Master Parker had fucked her!

Lynn said all it took to get him to fuck you was to sign some papers. It turned on Master Parker. He'd fuck you as soon as you signed them or even as you signed them. Which made them pretty hard to read or to remember what all was in them.

They were pretty long with a lot of words and Lynn was not exactly a reader. None of them were. At least, not any longer.

As best Lynn could figure it was about Master Parker being their Master. Which they already knew anyway. He could do whatever he wanted and they had to do whatever he said. Which, again, they already knew anyway.

Asking around none too subtly during work-outs (sometimes called "whip outs") with Violet she learned many – most! -- of the others had also been fucked – fucked with cock – by Master Parker. Always it was signing a bunch of papers that led to the fucking.

She knew it was strange how obsessed she was that Master Parker fuck her. She knew she hadn't found him attractive before. She knew he wasn't. Objectively. But nowadays he seemed like a living god to her. An average looking, undersized, nerdy, poorly dressed living god but, still, a living god to her.

What once she wanted nothing of she now obsessed to have.

So Penny formed a plan such as it was. Instead of yelling things like "I'm a filthy shoe slut, Master Parker" she would find a way to work in something like "I'm so horny I would sign anything, Master Parker". Just gasp it out maybe while riding his shoe. That might finally put the right wrong idea into Master Parker's head.

She knew she was just one more sexy slut to Master Parker but it was still so very important to her that he fuck her.

So she carried out her plan and it worked like a charm.

Almost as soon as she planted the seed she was bent over his desk trying to read some very small print while her vision went in and out of focus with each thrust home of his cock into her pussy.

All she could really care about was the success of her plan and her imminent orgasm. It was so important to her that she orgasm around his cock. So she quickly signed page after page with her unsteady hand, then braced her hands on the edges of the desk, and climaxed as he planted his own seed right into the depths of her pussy.

Things didn't seem to go so well for the team. The Rhinos won some games but lost more than they won. Rhinos was a great name for a team in a running league but a name did not make for overall success.

Penny wasn't sure how the coaches or players felt about things. The cheerleaders were not allowed to socialize with them. As in not one word allowed. Penny figured Mistress Violet and Master Parker were jealous of their territory or didn't want them to get knocked up. Probably both.

Of course, all the cheerleaders obeyed their directive. All of them were all about the obedience.

Besides the substandard play on the field the team was also doing poorly in ticket sales. There just weren't a lot of fans in the stands. Many more seats were empty than filled.

Oddly, the luxury boxes were all sold out. Status symbols for the rich. They did not really seem like real fans. Not of the players.

The rich luxury box owners and their retinues, cronies, and spoiled family members seemed to only come out of their boxes to come down and tour the sideline spending almost all their time getting up close looks at the fourteen cheerleaders.

Penny thought they studied them like they were some kind of... cattle. Or something. It was lustful but it was also evaluative. Like people appraising a valuable painting.

Valuable... but how valuable? Why?

Enjoyable... but in what way? Or ways?

Penny once overheard something Master Parker said. Something that seemed important. She thought Master Parker had sort of forgotten about her down there because she had her face on the sole of one shoe licking, had been there for quite some time, and the conversation he had on the phone was longer than usual.

She heard him say, "The ticket sales don't matter anyway. It's all one big tax write off. The way the tax laws are, and with multiple revenue streams, failure can be lucrative. Of course, we don't need to list the cheerleaders as an asset or report those profits. So its a money maker and a tax write off and tax free. Eat our cake and have it also and then eat it again."

She wondered about that later that night and from time to time as the season wore on. Didn't the cheerleaders help make profits by bringing fans into the building, pretty much just like the players? If they didn't get fans then weren't the players and the cheerleaders both failures?

Were they making money off cheerleader calendars or something? She couldn't even remember them posing for cheer team photos but a lot of things were a sexual blur. Hell, they may have all posed nude for all she knew. She often felt drunk on sex.

She figured the new living arrangements were a part of the cheer team helping the team save money. All fourteen of them were housed in one large old house and each shared a room. They slept in actual bunk-beds. Sleeping in bunk-beds was both sort of humiliating and sort of fun. It was like they were in the Army or at camp. The cheerleader army. Or cheerleader camp.

They didn't have to worry about room and board but then they were paid a lot less and their pay went into "retirement funds". Probably out of efficiency, the funds were run by Mr. Parker. He sure didn't like questions about the money. Got real cranky and you could never get an actual answer from him.

Violet also lived at the house. Of course, she had a huge bedroom with nice furniture. The walls were none too thick. At least, not thick enough when someone got spanked or whipped.

Most nights Violet would choose one of the cheerleaders for "bonus" training in her bedroom. When she stalked around the house peering from one to the next making her choice everyone tensed with a combination of nervous dread and anticipation. They were either going to get used until weary with passion and pain or... not.

You could actually smell the pussy fumes increase in the closed space of the big house while Violet paced about narrowing her eyes and making her selection.

Violet didn't sleep much and she kept her selection up all night. Or selections if she chose more than one cheerleader as she often did. Being "trained" by her. Which meant spanks to "tone" them, whippings to "help them learn", lots and lots of sex to "exercise" them. A whole lot of tongue exercising as well!

Even once Violet fell asleep her choice of cheerleader was required to stay standing next to her bed. It was total sleep deprivation with no relief the next day. It wasn't easy to stand all night quietly either. But it was great exercise for the legs. All the girls had to at least admit that. It also wasn't easy to stay quiet standing there as you masturbated to an orgasm. It was boring so what else could you do?

Violet did a pretty good job of rotating them on this special training. Each selection, even after they finally caught up on their sleep days later, seemed even more subdued, submissive, and obedient than they already were.

It worked the same way on Penny. She noticed it working on her. She felt it working on her. She... accepted it. That was just one way that it was working on her. Making her accept... just whatever.

No one really truly refused anything. Just some hesitations to obey at times due to dismay at what they were told to do. Those hesitations, just that, would usually lead to a "no slumber slumber party" with Violet as the cheerleaders privately called them. That, in turn, led to a dramatic reduction in hesitations.

After months of this all fourteen of them would do anything they were told. Anything. Right away.

In order to help them focus on their cheerleader careers they also had to cut off contact with friends and family. That didn't mean just not calling or visiting them. Or, heaven forbid – heaven being Violet – a friend or family member visiting one of them at the old house. No, no!

The old house was a secret. The secret had to be protected. That was why they also never went out shopping or to the bars or... out anywhere but the stadium.

Each cheerleader actually had to alienate their family and friends so there was no risk of intrusion or distraction. They did this by phone with Violet standing quietly next to them with arms crossed, tapping her foot, and with a hard look on her face.

They always used Violet's phone and, once the friends and family were cut off, Violet took their own cell phones and cut service to them. Had to protect the secret of the old house.

Violet liked to say, "Loose lips sink ships. And loose lips should be let loose on pussy instead."

Once the family and friends were fully alienated the cheerleader could really focus on her cheer career. Violet liked to say sacrifices had to be made and she was happy to sacrifice everyone's family and friends.

The last game of the year was a home game. They never traveled with the team to away games but stayed behind doing extra training. There was excitement in the air. Not about the year's won/loss total. The Rhinos were out of playoff contention weeks before.

The excitement was due to the prospect of change. They all supposed they would need to go find new jobs and new places to live and maybe mend fences with family and friends. No one looked forward to any of that but it was still exciting. Change was in the air.

Being a cheerleader was not a full year gig they assumed.

The excitement also projected from Mistress Violet and Master Parker. Mistress Violent seemed even more on edge and alert than usual. She was always pretty wired but much more so the day of the last game.

Master Parker came down to their little locker area and even gave a short speech about the importance of service and serving. That if you could not be a noble the most noble you could be was to serve a noble. That lessors serving betters was the natural course of life. He went off on a tangent about social evolution, whatever that was.

It was weird him talking to them about nobility after the way he treated them in such an ignoble way.

Yes. Change was in the air.

The game was listless. Both teams, out of playoff contention, seemed to play halfhearted. Word was the league was going to disband after one year. Maybe, maybe not.

The Rhinos actually won, 13-7.

The rich luxury box owners and their companions were more active than usual. Coming down to the railing. Whether males or females they seemed like perverts as they stared at the cheerleaders and seemed almost unaware a game was going on.

Penny realized she shouldn't call, or even think of, anyone else being a pervert what with her being a well-practiced shoe slut and all around slut.

The rich luxury box owners all came down to the sidelines at various times. All of them. Which had never happened before. Penny thought maybe they were trying to get their monies worth.

Penny wasn't sure how much one of those luxury boxes cost but, whatever they paid, they had not gotten their monies worth so far. Still wouldn't no matter how much they ogled the cheerleaders.

Penny, while dancing and prancing and cheering in her scandalously skimpy outfit, noticed she received a lot of attention from these visitors. It was both creepy and complimentary. She had learned she liked to be stared at as a sexual object. It made her hot. The way it made her feel and the thoughts that ran through her head would have scandalized a women's libber. Or Penny from half a year earlier.

One couple in particular paid her a lot of attention. At least, she thought they were a couple. A really old guy with a big gut. He was probably 70. The other one seemed like some kind of trophy wife. A skinny blonde with a pinched face who might not be able to get into a bar legally.

She wasn't exactly ugly but she'd never have made the cheer team. Still, a wife like that, if she was his wife, was a big win for the old guy.

They kept watching her, talking, laughing sometimes, pointing at her. Nodding in agreement.

When the game ended they disappeared. She wondered if they would perhaps think about her when they next had sex.

She was glad she didn't have sex with those types of people.

Not just due to age and appearance.

She could tell they had an arrogant privileged attitude like they deserved to be rich and the poor deserved to be poor. Everyone knew the rich were the real entitled. Then they ran around bitching about people trying to get health insurance or, you know, trying not starve to death after retiring.

After the game Mistress Violet told each of them to go to an assigned luxury box for post-game entertainment.

Something with the look in Mistress Violet's eyes.

Penny had a feeling about this. A bad feeling. The feeling you get when you know an asteroid is about to strike the city you are currently in the middle of while stuck in a traffic jam.

Penny dutifully went to her assigned luxury box, 2E.

Was she surprised to see that odd couple of the old guy and the skinny young blonde?

No. Not at all.

Was she surprised when they told her she now belonged to them?   Yes. Quite a bit.

In fact, she really didn't believe it. She even went so far as to dare to let them know that.

She did not appreciate it when the old guy used a surprisingly strong grip with a handful of hair to bend her over the white-tiled mini-bar. She certainly didn't appreciate it when the blonde spanked her.

She wasn't sure what to do about all that. The customer was always right and she'd been told by Mistress Violet and by Master Parker all the fans were customers but *especially* the luxury box owners were.

The skinny girl could really swing her open palm and Penny was sure the leather gloves she wore made the spanks worse as well. Even when her ass was blazing from the spanks she still tried to make clear she did not *belong* to them.

She didn't say it but, maybe... if they wanted to have her sexually as a post-game celebration... well, Master Parker and Mistress Violet would probably be proud of her. Plus, her pussy was nearly as hot already as her spanked ass!

The blonde left her rear and placed some papers on the mini-bar in front of her face. It was hard to read that small print.

Hey, that small print looked familiar!

Her tight performance shorts sliding down her legs also felt quite familiar. That old guy wasn't afraid to help himself. The cooled air felt refreshing on her hot ass. Even as her ass cooled her pussy flame rose higher. Being exposed like this to the old guy was so wrong and wicked.

The blonde pointed at sections of the papers as she flipped through them and made Penny observe some of her own signatures. They were pretty unsteady and wavy. She recalled she'd been under the influence of passion at the time.

Would that be cause to claim in court the signatures weren't binding? Didn't matter. She had no money for a lawyer.

And not much will to resist anyone or anything either.

She felt a cock slide home in her hot wet pussy sleeve. The feeling was welcome and she felt gentled like a baby given a pacifier. Though, of course, it was her pussy clinging to that big cock, not her mouth. She was surprised. The old guy's cock was quite hard and bigger than you'd think for a guy his size. Old people shrank, right? Maybe their naughty parts stayed the same size while they shrunk.

That or maybe he was rich enough to have had some kind of surgical penis enhancement. That must be what it was.

She never would have thought she'd get fucked by a seventy-year-old until she was at least sixty. She was thirty-two years ahead of that expectation.

The old guy's thrusts were purposely staccato. Each time the skinny young bitch pointed to one of Penny's signatures or pointed to a particular line to make a point about what was required of Penny the old guy pushed his unnaturally big cock all the way in.

Penny knew he was trying to create association in her between her newfound full-on slavery to them and pleasure. Mistress Violet and Master Parker did plenty of that sort of thing to her.

Penny figured the pleasure association trick was totally unnecessary.

Because the contract was clear and the pleasure was tremendous. She was theirs. She belonged to them. They could do as they wanted with her. She had to obey all commands or even suggestions. She could not do anything without their permission. Not even go to the bathroom!

When the blonde got to the end where Mr. Parker had signed his ownership of Penny over to the old guy – who she saw was named Winston Bigelow – the old guy, Mr. Bigelow, or, she guessed, Master Bigelow, went into a thrusting frenzy that left her breathless even before her orgasm struck. Which it did, big time, more or less right as he shot off deep inside her.

She was so effected she even drooled a little on the contract. Great, now they'd think she was even stupider than your average dumb slut. She reread the end and saw that Master Parker, to be specific, had sold her to Winston Bigelow and heirs.

Huh. So even once the old guy... Master Bigelow... died she would still be a slave? To who, his eldest son or something?

The blonde told her to thank her new owner and Master for the honor of receiving his sperm.

"Thank you, sir. Thank you, Master Bigelow."

He grunted acknowledgment. Then he sat down heavily. He didn't seem like he was in very good shape. She might meet the heir fairly soon.

Little did she know.

The nasty blonde addressed her, "I'm sure reading those words has strained your mind. Time for you to relax and do what you're good at. Lick my pussy, slave."

There wasn't much Penny could say to that. She knew she had indeed gotten pretty good at pussy licking. Too bad this one would be enjoying the fruits of all her hard training. She watched the young woman strip and sit on top of the mini-bar with legs spread wide.

"Get to it."

Penny did.

Should or shouldn't, she liked it. Liked her taste. Liked the way she was exploited and the way she submissively allowed herself to do as ordered. Liked it? Loved it actually. She made sure the young woman liked what she was doing. For some reason she felt grateful for the opportunity to go down on her and wanted to show the little bitch her gratitude.

After a lot of effort doing her best tongue and mouth work trying to please the bitch she felt a light spank on her rear. Old man Bigelow was up and moving.

"Do you like servicing your better's pussy?"

What to say? If in doubt, tell the truth, "Yes, Master Bigelow, I like licking your wife's pussy."

He laughed so hard he began coughing hard. The bitch was laughing also.

Master Bigelow was too busy hacking up a lung so the bitch spoke for him, "Stupid slave, I'm not his wife. I'm his granddaughter."

What to say to that!?! Going back to licking pussy gave her a good reason to say nothing.

The bitch – granddaughter Bigelow – was soon quite close to orgasm as her grandfather looked on paternally. Or, Penny guessed, grand-paternally.

It seemed the bitch wanted to imprint a few more rules and expectations on Penny. She issued them sentence by sentence as Penny strove with all her mighty tongue to make her orgasm. Just to maybe shut her up.

"You can call me Mistress Bigelow."

Lick. Lick. Lick.

"When Grampa passes away – hopefully not until he's a hundred, of course – you will be all mine."

Lick. Lick. Lick.

"My parents are... no longer in the picture... so I am Grampa's direct heir."

Lick. Lick. Lick.

"We have our own island which helps us maintain our privacy and to avoid legal issues."

Lick. Lick. Lick.

"I'd like to say the island keeps the riffraff out but... I can't as you and other slaves will be on the island, after all."

Lick. Lick. Lick.

"I read in the report on you that you are concerned about the size of your breasts."

Lick. Lick. Lick.

"You don't have to worry about the size of your breasts any longer."

Lick. Lick. Lick.

"Right away, soon as possible, we will have them greatly augmented surgically."

Lick. Lick. Lick!

"Don't worry, your tits will be much much larger soon."

Lick! Lick! Lick!

Appalled, Penny almost stopped pussy-licking. Almost, but her task was too important to abandon. In fact, somehow she licked harder.

Perhaps to encourage her, Master Bigelow penetrated her with his cock. He was already hard again? Breathtaking! Doubtless he had some chemical help of some sort. Still. Prodigious.

His cock in her hot needy pussy also felt wondrous.

Young Mistress Bigelow got breathless as she neared orgasm. She could still talk though and Penny could still understand her even with the girl's thighs clamped to her ears.

"You will have many opportunities to show us your gratitude for taking you away from your mundane life among the poor. You'll serve us sexually, obviously, but also your experience as a waitress was a selling point – or, for us, a purchasing point – as you will have ample opportunities to serve us and our numerous guests. Both food and sex. Sometimes at the same time."

Master Bigelow grunted and groaned an addendum to her prognostication, "Shoe, boot, sandal, and various footwear cleaning with your slave mouth in addition. You will be a sort of sexual coat check girl but with footwear instead of coats."

Penny could picture it. Picture it all. Destiny. Like it had all already happened and she just needed to play it out once again.

Penny was surprised when she was the first to orgasm. Mistress Bigelow followed moments later crushing Penny's face against her pussy. Master Bigelow then blew a second load into her pussy which intensified her orgasm.

Ten minutes later, once they were all recovered to varying degrees, they got dressed. Penny politely waited until she was told to get dressed. Then Mistress Bigelow told her to carry her huge purse and Master Bigelow's briefcase out to the limo.

Mistress Bigelow told her she'd be expected to complete any and many tasks in service to her owners. To serve and service in any and all ways.

Penny realized she'd come full circle.

She'd became a cheerleader to escape the long nights as a waitress in the service industry.

But here she was now... right back in the service industry!

The End

Also now available by Jordan Church:

Cheerleader In Trouble

Book Description

Addison is a cheerleader at her college and is concerned one of her fellow cheerleaders is in trouble and is being sexually dominated by a male assistant to the team. Addison tells the coach, an older lady, who does not seem to take the concern seriously but who knows more about it than she lets on.

Addison decides she must do something to help. She will prove what the dominant male is doing to her friend. But will her efforts save her friend or only prove Addison is like her friend and that she, too, would like to be dominated, spanked, humiliated, used, abused, and made to orgasm repeatedly?

If (when) Addison is caught sneaking around trying to help, who will really be in the most trouble, her beautiful friend or sexy Addison?

Addison begins an unexpected journey of self-discovery regarding BDSM, punishment, domination and submission, orgy, spanking, and lesbian action. Will she like having a Master and a Mistress or will she rebel? Will her goodness and her values save her from becoming a submissive?

Cheerleader In Trouble

Did the idea of the twisted thing they'd done, that sexual prank at her expense, turn her on? It did. It shouldn't, of course, but... it did. They probably laughed at her. It probably aroused them what they did to her.

She suddenly hated them. But she couldn't fully blame them. Even she was turned on by what they'd done to her.

All this was just so bizarre. She'd never heard of this kind of thing or seen any porn like it, not that she watched much porn. She'd had no exposure. So she had no resistance.

Delbert's cock was hard again and he moved close behind Mandy still bent over Ms. Felton's desk, "Punishment over. We'll see what happens this week with masturbating in front of your roommate and cum-hugging Mari and Addison. For now, I'll just fuck your ass."

"Yes, Master Delbert, please do fuck my ass."

No, Mandy! Don't do it! Not the ass. Never the ass! To what purpose? Gross. Don't do it!

Mandy either did not hear Addison's mental plea or ignored it. Mandy held still except for moaning louder and louder as he pressed in.

Addison would never want to be ass fucked but, she had to admit, it was quite arousing to see someone else give up their ass to their "Master". Addison's right hand went right back at it. Trying to rub her pussy juice right back into her pussy. It wouldn't work. But it sure felt great trying.

Addison continued to hold her recording phone out to capture the scene. She no longer thought she'd need it to prove mistreatment by Delbert towards Mandy. Clearly he was mistreating her but clearly she didn't mind it. As long as "didn't mind" actually meant "was into it".

If she ever used the video it would be to watch it in private while she masturbated.

What was she going to do this week? Let Mandy hug her with dried cum on her uniform and act like nothing? Even that idea turned her on.

Long wonderful minutes passed as Delbert ass fucked Mandy. Mandy gripped the desk and took it like a sexual heroine in Addison's eyes. Sexual heroine? There she went again thinking inappropriately about this.

Addison jammed her fingers in her pussy. She noticed that she instinctively thrust them in time with Delbert's thrusts into Mandy's ass. It was almost like her fingers in her pussy were Delbert's cock. A terrible thought. Terribly arousing.

Ms. Felton was totally wrong earlier about Addison being at all jealous. Wrong then but she'd be right if she said it again now. Not jealous of being ass fucked or having sex with Delbert. But jealous of her access to and use of Delbert's cock? Yes. That.

Addison's world narrowed to riding her own hand and a sort of tunnel vision watching the sexual display in front of her.

But suddenly her world expanded.

A hand grabbed Addison's smart phone out of her extended hand. Simultaneously, another hand grabbed a handful of blonde hair at the back of Addison's head. Used it to twist Addison's head around....

Questions, complaints, or suggestions?

Feel free to contact me: jordanchurch@mail.com

See what I have available and my author bio (such as it is) and photo (such as it is) at

amazon.com/author/jordanchurch

Sign up for my newsletter to be notified of new releases as they occur. No waiting and wondering, just

waiting! Also includes a sample scene from each new release for your enjoyment. Ctrl-click to open a

hyperlink:

http://tinyletter.com/Jordan8Church

Printed in Great Britain
by Amazon

43259634R00108